"Hello, Cam,"

Hallie said as he neared the porch.

Cam's breath stopped for just a second, at the sight of Hallie. Her hair was tucked up and held in place with a tortoiseshell comb, but wispy tendrils escaped here and there and teased at the blush on her cheeks.

She'd changed into a pair of white shorts that made her legs look a good mile longer than they already were, and all too shapely for his peace of mind. Her top was a pretty shade of mint—and made her green eyes look big and wide in the evening twilight. If he'd ever wanted to touch a woman, it was this woman…at this moment.

But what about forever?

Dear Reader,

March roars in like a lion at Silhouette Romance, starting with popular author Susan Meier and *Husband from 9 to 5,* her exciting contribution to LOVING THE BOSS, a six-book series in which office romance leads to happily-ever-after. In this sparkling story, a bump on the head has a boss-loving woman believing she's married to the man of her dreams....

In March 1998, beloved author Diana Palmer launched VIRGIN BRIDES. This month, *Callaghan's Bride* not only marks the anniversary of this special Romance promotion, but it continues her wildly successful LONG, TALL TEXANS series! As a rule, hard-edged, hard-bodied Callaghan Hart distrusted sweet, virginal, starry-eyed young ladies. But ranch cook Tess Brady had this cowboy hankerin' to break all his rules.

Judy Christenberry's LUCKY CHARM SISTERS miniseries resumes with a warm, emotional pretend engagement story that might just lead to *A Ring for Cinderella.* When a jaded attorney delivers a very pregnant stranger's baby, he starts a journey toward healing...and making this woman his *Texas Bride,* the heartwarming new novel by Kate Thomas. In *Soldier and the Society Girl* by Vivian Leiber, the month's HE'S MY HERO selection, sparks fly when a true-blue, true-grit American hero requires the protocol services of a refined blue blood. A lone-wolf lawman meets his match in an indomitable schoolteacher—and her moonshining granny—in Gayle Kaye's *Sheriff Takes a Bride,* part of FAMILY MATTERS.

Enjoy this month's fantastic offerings, and make sure to return each and every month to Silhouette Romance!

Mary-Theresa Hussey

Mary-Theresa Hussey
Senior Editor, Silhouette Romance

Please address questions and book requests to:
Silhouette Reader Service
U.S.: 3010 Walden Ave., P.O. Box 1325, Buffalo, NY 14269
Canadian: P.O. Box 609, Fort Erie, Ont. L2A 5X3

SHERIFF
TAKES A BRIDE

Gayle Kaye

Published by Silhouette Books

America's Publisher of Contemporary Romance

To the Gopher Girls,
Mary, Zeidi and the one
who always got caught

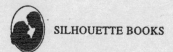 SILHOUETTE BOOKS

ISBN 0-373-19359-9

SHERIFF TAKES A BRIDE

This edition published by arrangement with Harlequin Books S.A.

® and TM are trademarks of Harlequin Books S.A., used under license. Trademarks indicated with ® are registered in the United States Patent and Trademark Office, the Canadian Trade Marks Office and in other countries.

Printed in U.S.A.

Books by Gayle Kaye

Silhouette Romance

Hard Hat and Lace #925
His Delicate Condition #961
Daddy Trouble #1014
Bachelor Cop #1177
Daddyhood #1227
Sheriff Takes a Bride #1359

GAYLE KAYE

lives in Kansas City, Missouri, and finds the Midwest a rich setting for romance novels. Her first romance in 1989 reached the finals of the Romance Writers of America Golden Heart contest; a second was nominated by *Romantic Times Magazine* as Best Silhouette Romance of the year. A wife, a mom, a nurse, she draws from many life experiences for her ideas. Her passions include her husband, her kids, traveling, reading and, of course, writing romances.

Gayle loves to hear from her readers. You can write to her at P.O. Box 29275, Parkville, MO 64152.

Dear Reader,

I was excited to learn *Sheriff Takes a Bride* is part of Silhouette's new promotion, FAMILY MATTERS. Families today can be far from the typical family of the "Leave It to Beaver" days, but the key ingredient remains: love. In all my stories love abounds, love accomplishes, love encourages and love protects.

I believe in the power of family relationships. I can draw from my own experience as a single mom raising two daughters and finally meeting my very own Prince Charming, of the hardships endured and the love that was gained. I've written about these single moms, giving them their own unique stories.

We all have a cherished family member, one in whom we can put our trust, one who nurtures and encourages us. For Hallie Cates in *Sheriff Takes a Bride* that person is her independent and often cantankerous grandmother. Hallie has her job cut out for her trying to corral the moonshining Granny Pearl—and it doesn't help that the local sheriff, Cam Osborne, has arrested the woman for her illicit trade. Or that he believes Hallie is involved.

Family means everything to Hallie and, in its own way, to Cam. But can love prevail between the two of them? It takes Granny Pearl to see that they have "family" potential.

Gayle Kaye

Chapter One

"Hallie, I need you. You gotta come."

Hallie Cates had never heard such a tremor in Granny Pearl's voice before. Her grandmother was headstrongly in charge of her own life. Always. Something was definitely wrong.

Hallie abandoned the cookies she'd just taken from the oven and shifted the phone on her shoulder. "Granny Pearl, what is it? Are you all right?"

"No—I'm far from all right. In fact, I might never be all right again."

There. Hallie heard the old familiar spunk she always associated with Granny Pearl. She drew an easier breath, if only for the moment. The seventy-nine-year-old woman lived all alone, tucked away in tiny, *backwards*—to Hallie's way of thinking, Greens Hollow, Arkansas, but it was home to Granny Pearl. And the old girl vehemently refused to budge from there.

"I wouldn't call you if it wasn't important, Hallie." The woman snuffled. Or maybe it was the scratchiness of the phone system in the Ozark hill country.

"You know you can call me anytime, Granny Pearl. Now, calm down and tell me what it is."

Granny could take care of herself, even reveled in the fact, claimed she'd be carried out of her cabin feet first and no other way. And Hallie wasn't sure she could change her mind on that score. Still, she worried about her relative.

"This...horrible cuss of a varmint has arrested me. Locked me up and won't let me go home. I need to feed George and Myrtle."

Granny's voice quavered again at the last. Hallie heard it, knew her grandmother would be upset to be away from her two pesky goats, but she suspected the animals would somehow survive. It was Granny Pearl she was concerned about.

"*Arrested?* Granny, there must be some mistake." Who would arrest a harmless little old lady, and for what? Jaywalking across the town's lone hilly street that saw maybe four cars and six dogs in the way of traffic in any twenty-four hour period?

"He's locked me up and throwed away the key. I'm sure he means to feed me bread and water for supper—*if* I even get supper."

Granny's voice sounded strong. And mad. Hallie took that as a good sign. When Granny Pearl got her dander up, the earth shook around her. In fact, maybe Hallie should have a little charitable pity for the poor sheriff.

"Let me talk to Sheriff Potts, Granny Pearl." Hallie would settle this.

"It's not Sheriff Potts. We buried him six months ago. This...varmint's a new breed. And not from these parts."

Hallie was sorry to hear about Virgil Potts. She remembered him from summers she'd spent with Granny in Greens Hollow. "Then let me talk to this new var—*man*," she said, correcting herself. "I'm sure I can straighten everything out."

Granny laid the phone down. Hallie heard a quick, muffled conversation, complete with a little ripe cussing from Granny Pearl, then a deep male voice came on the line.

There was nothing scratchy about the phone line now. It fairly rumbled with the low, earthy voice. Hallie felt it tingle across her nerve endings like sandpaper over new skin. She drew a deep breath and squared her shoulders. "Sheriff," she said coolly, "just what is it my grandmother's supposed to have done?"

Sheriff Cam Osborne heard the tension in Hallie Cates's voice ripple across the wire. He couldn't help but wonder if the woman was the she-lion her granny was. And what the granddaughter from Fort Worth would say if she knew Granny Pearl had sunk her teeth into his right arm in a moment of nonvigilance on his part. *That* was a mistake he wasn't about to make again—even if he had to lock the old gal up in solitary until her temper cooled a bit. *If* it ever did.

It would probably be one cold day in hell.

"She's been charged with a couple of things, the

most serious being selling moonshine to half the
county." He'd keep the resisting arrest and assaulting an officer of the law with a seventy-nine-year-
old set of choppers for later. At least until he knew
what kind of woman Pearl Cates's pretty granddaughter was. He hated to admit he was interested.
He'd seen her picture standing in a frame on the
mantel over Granny's fireplace. Thick red hair, worn
loose to her shoulders, high blushing cheekbones and
a sweet little mouth that just begged to be kissed.

But that he knew he had no business thinking
about. Who even knew if Hallie Cates would come
to her grandmother's rescue? Hadn't Pearl said her
granddaughter didn't come back to Arkansas very
often?

He took some vague satisfaction at her small gasp.
"Moonshine? Why…why Granny Pearl would
never… She wouldn't… I mean, Sheriff, there must
be some *mistake.*"

And she clearly implied he'd made it. Cam sniffed
the cork of the hundred-proof "evidence" he'd confiscated from his prisoner, nearly becoming looped
from the stuff's fumes. Oh, the old woman was
guilty all right. Not to mention, downright unrepen-
tant about her little…business. "Trust me, Ms.
Cates, there's been no mistake."

Another small gasp, this one sounding more like
an irate sigh. "How could you even *think* one sweet,
docile, little old lady would break the law? Why,
Granny is—"

"Neither sweet, nor docile," he interrupted the
tirade she was only just warming to. From her spot
beside him, Granny Pearl was giving him the devil

eye. The woman was just lucky he hadn't handcuffed her to that chair she was sitting on. No, she was hardly sweet. And as for docile…?

He rubbed the bite mark on his arm.

"Okay, okay, so Granny may be a little…*feisty*," Hallie Cates admitted from her end of the line. "But she's as honest and law-abiding as the day is long. And I can vouch for that."

Cam dragged a hand through his dark hair. They were getting nowhere here. "I'm sure you'll get an opportunity to voice your opinion in court," he told her, "but for now—"

Cam had to hold the phone away from his ear. "Just what kind of a low-down poleskunk are you to throw a little old lady in the clink and feed her nothing but bread and water for supper?" The woman's blast was nearly deafening.

"Give him hell, Hallie!" Granny yelped, joining in the fracas from this end. She'd gotten to her feet and was threatening Cam with balled fists.

It wouldn't take much for him to lock both women in a cell for a year or two. What had ever made him think a job as small-town sheriff might be preferable to the vicissitudes of the Chicago police force? He had to be crazy.

No—he wasn't. It was the world. The world was crazy. Here, *everywhere*. He'd only thought he'd escaped it.

Cam didn't relish the reputation he was sure to get for locking up a seventy-nine-year-old, and a woman, at that. But the law was the law. And Cam didn't bend it. Not in Chicago—and not here.

"Well, Sheriff?"

Cam ordered Pearl back to her chair, then returned his attention to the voice on the other end. He suspected under other circumstances it could be velvety, caressing a man's soul, not to mention his well-fired hormones. "The menu tonight is planked steak and green beans, with a side of biscuits. And I might suggest you don't believe everything your sweet little grandmother tells you, Ms. Cates."

It was all Cam could say at the moment. He didn't know what the hell he was going to do with Pearl Cates. Or with her granddaughter, who would no doubt be showing up soon, wrapped in plenty of fury and indignation, to save Pearl from the town's heartless sheriff.

Hallie hated driving the winding back roads that led to Greens Hollow. At night they were much more than winding, they were downright dangerous. But the rude, *unfeeling* sheriff had left her no choice but to drop everything and race to the small town. That was, unless she wanted Granny to be spending a night alone in jail, at the man's mercy—something of which Sheriff Cam Osborne had little, if any, she suspected.

She'd hastily thrown clothes into a suitcase, wrapped up the cookies she'd baked, deciding to take them to Granny, and headed off down the highway.

School was out for the summer, and her class of second-graders would be going off to camp, swimming, having fun—and Hallie would miss them. She'd planned a full summer schedule for herself as well, one that hadn't included bailing her grand-mother out of jail.

She'd intended to try her hand at tennis lessons, read a few books she'd been saving for a lazy sunny afternoon on the side porch, maybe take a language course—Russian or Eastern Tibetan—whatever struck her fancy.

But Granny Pearl needed her.

It was ten o'clock by the time Hallie drew up in front of the sheriff's office. It was a small stone building that had been around for at least half a century, newer than most of the places in or around Greens Hollow. Every light inside was blazing, which meant that Cam Osborne hadn't locked Granny in for the night and gone home, leaving the old woman alone and frightened.

If he had, he'd have had to answer to Hallie.

Hallie slammed the door to her small, overheated red Subaru, trying to keep her mind on rescuing Granny. If only the old girl would move to Fort Worth with her, it would make Hallie's life simpler, she thought as she hurried toward the front entrance.

"*Cheating?* I am *not* cheating! *You,* Sheriff, are wrong. *I never cheat.*"

"Or make moonshine either, I suppose?"

Hallie recognized the deep resonant voice follow-ing Granny's as the one she'd heard earlier on the phone.

A checkers game was in hot progress through the cell bars, Granny on the unfortunate side of them. Hallie stood and stared, curious to see if Granny could hold her own against the man who held her captive, both literally and otherwise.

"I saw you move that checker, you sneaky old woman—and you're not going to get away with it," came the sheriff's reply.

"Prove it, Cam Osborne!"

Hallie hid a smile at Granny's ornery rejoinder and wondered if the man would back down. He didn't look the type to do any such thing. She took in the width of his shoulders. Unless she missed her guess, the man could wrestle a bear as easily as he could a little old lady who cheated at checkers. Maybe, just maybe, Granny had met her match with Cam Osborne.

His long legs were stretched out in front of him, sheathed in faded denim that fit him like a second skin. His shirt was a dusky blue and fit him just as sensually. Thick dark hair, worn a little long, curled over his shirt collar, and Hallie found herself wondering at its silkiness, what it might be like to delve her fingers into its richness. Quickly she checked that thought.

"Game's over, Granny." He folded the game board, sending checkers flying.

There was a spate of cussing from Granny before she spotted Hallie over the man's broad shoulders.

"Hallie! Thank God you're here. This brute is no gentleman."

"And you, Pearl Cates, are no lady."

Ignoring Granny's loud harumph, he turned toward Hallie and stuck out a hand. "Sheriff Cam Osborne," he said.

Hallie glanced at the man's hand, debating about taking it. It was broad and sensual. Capable. Of what, she didn't want to think about. It would swallow hers up without a doubt and she'd feel the tingle all the way to her toes. And she wasn't sure she should risk that—not at the moment. If she were wise, not ever.

"Sheriff," she said coolly.

The man's eyes were a beguiling brown, his jaw strong and slightly arrogant, the kind that invited a fight or two on a Saturday night—and she didn't have to guess who would come out the winner. His smile was slow and tempting when he chose to let it slip.

"I want out of here, Hallie. Tell this man to let me go." Granny had her wizened face pressed to the bars, and Hallie had the sense that if the woman could get her hands on Cam Osborne at the moment she'd let loose with one good roundhouse punch.

Not that it would have a whole lot of impact on that granite body of his.

"I intend to do just that, Granny," Hallie said, then ignoring the sheriff, went to give her grandmother a big warm hug, albeit through the cell bars.

"I brought you your favorite cookies, Granny," she told the woman and saw a smile light her face.

"Bring 'em to me now," she said. "That supper I got wasn't enough to feed a carrier pigeon. I'm starved."

"They're out in my car. I'll get them," Hallie said.

When she returned with the plate of cookies wrapped in aluminum foil the sheriff had other ideas. "I, uh, need to check those before you hand them over to my...prisoner," he said.

Hallie rolled her eyes. "Aw, come on, Sheriff, you

think I baked a hacksaw blade in one of these little chocolate chippers?''

A slight smile touched his sexy mouth. ''Where a Cates is concerned, a man can't be too careful.''

Hallie handed him the plate and waited indignantly while he peeled back the foil. ''I suppose they look safe enough.'' He took one from the plate and popped it into his mouth.

''Well, Sheriff, if you didn't bite into anything that will saw through bars, may I give these to my grandmother?''

He waved a hand magnanimously. ''Be my guest.''

The nerve of the man, suspecting her of subterfuge, suspecting Granny of…anything, and locking the poor soul up like she was some…common criminal.

''Hallie, you do make the best cookies,'' Granny said and took a fistful as if she might never get another morsel of food.

The dear probably thought she'd never again see the light of day, either. And that was a situation Hallie intended to remedy—and fast. ''Excuse me, Granny Pearl. I have a few things to say to the sheriff.''

''Go get him, Hallie!'' Granny said and snatched the entire plate from Hallie's hands.

Not the best move. She might have been able to use the cookies as a bargaining tool in demanding Granny's release. Now she'd have to depend on the man's *reasonable* side—providing he had one.

She approached his desk and sat down in the lone chair beside it, crossing one jean-clad leg over the other. Her foot and leg pumped, revealing her nervousness. She'd never tried to bargain with the law before, not even over a speeding ticket.

She supposed anger wouldn't work, though she had a lot of it. She suspected wheedling would get her nowhere either, and she'd never been very good at that anyway. Reason—it was the only thing worth attempting.

"Sheriff..." Hallie struggled for calm. "I—I'm sure we can work this out if we discuss it like two sane, sensible people." She smiled as if to say, she'd try if he would.

"Batting those eyes isn't going to get you anywhere, Ms. Cates," he said superiorly. "Neither will flashing that pretty smile at me, delightful though it may be."

"Why, of all the arrogant—! I did not bat my eyes. And my smile, Cam Osborne, was an attempt at graciousness. Obviously that's something you wouldn't recognize if it jumped up and bit you on your backside," she retorted, her hackles up and on alert.

He grinned at that and Hallie wriggled in the chair. Damn, his office was close, *stuffy*. She wanted to throw open a window, take off a layer or two of clothing, except that she was wearing the minimum—jeans and a lightweight turtleneck top.

But she refused to let the man see her sweat. Or blush. Unfortunately she could control neither.

"I demand to know what proof you have against my grandmother," she said crisply.

"Uh, Hallie..." Granny called from the cell doors behind Hallie's chair.

"Not now, Granny Pearl. The sheriff and I are discussing…evidence."

"But, Hallie…"

Hallie ignored the warning tone in Granny Pearl's voice. A mistake, she realized when she saw the smug smile displayed on Cam's lips. He rocked back in his big chair, entirely too sure of himself.

"Proof, Ms. Cates?" he asked, definitely baiting her.

Hallie felt a slow trickle of perspiration zigzag its way into her cleavage. She had the distinct feeling she'd played right into the man's hands. Was that what Granny Pearl had been trying to tell her? Was that feisty, ornery little old woman guilty after all?

No, Hallie wouldn't believe it.

The man lowered the front legs of his chair to the floor with enough force to splinter wood. He reached for the lower desk drawer and yanked it open. "*Proof*, Ms. Cates," he said, extracting a jug of some sort from its interior.

The jug was tucked neatly inside a plastic bag, but even through the plastic Hallie could smell the contents.

Cam smiled. The woman seated beside his desk was turning a lovely shade of pink, and he found her intriguing. That signaled danger—danger he'd do well to heed. She was prettier than her picture, he decided. Much prettier, in a fragile, don't touch sort of way. And damned if he didn't want to touch.

Her long red locks fell in soft curls to her shoulders, tumbling in a too-tempting array of sun-kissed color. And scented—like warm outdoors, with a hint of apple blossoms. God, but he was sounding like a sentimental idiot. Maybe he'd been away from the harsh city streets too long; he was getting soft around the edges.

That had not been his plan when he'd left his past behind. He needed to maintain his edge, that hard streak he'd learned so well back in Chicago. Hell, the edge he'd been *born* with. It would be a real joke to be taken down by one tall, leggy woman, no matter how gorgeous she was.

Still, the look on Hallie Cates's face told Cam *she* was the one who was vulnerable at the moment. He saw the shadow of doubt that drew her well-shaped eyebrows together in a frown of worry when he'd produced the "evidence", the soft wrinkle of her nose at the smell emanating from the bottle he'd confiscated from Granny's well-hidden still. He had Pearl Cates dead to rights.

Hallie stiffened in her chair and directed her pretty gaze at him. "I'm sure there's some explanation, a reasonable one, one that will clear Granny of your so-called charges," she said, though with more bravado than conviction to her voice.

Cam found himself feeling sorry for her. He cast a glance at Pearl who paced the floor of her cell, chewing on a fingernail. He only hoped she bit all ten to a nub before she got the peevish idea to rake those nails across his face. The woman was wicked, he already knew from her bite, and he rubbed the spot on his arm as a reminder not to tangle with the wiry five-foot-two woman in the future.

The gesture caught Hallie's attention and she stared down at his injury, just below his rolled-up shirtsleeve. "What happened to your arm?" she asked with curiosity mingled with a certain wariness. "Those...those look like teeth marks."

"And every one of 'em are mine," Granny announced proudly from her cell. "How many seventy-year-olds can boast of having a full set?"

Just his luck the old woman did. "Your age, Pearl, is seventy-*nine*, not seventy," Cam reminded. He couldn't resist a smile at Hallie's mouth, which had closed with surprise at Granny's admission.

"I—I'm sorry, sorry about the...bite," she said quietly, chagrined. "I can't imagine what possessed her to...to..."

"Forget it," he answered. "The old gal got the better of me. It's not something that happens often."

His words were a warning, Hallie suspected. The man was tough, down to his very last well-hewn muscle. She was curious what he was doing in these parts. No one came here unless they'd been born and raised in these mountains. The place was isolated, not to mention backwards, full of gossip. Hallie had only just gotten here, and already she was anxious to get back to Fort Worth. That was, after she cleared Granny Pearl, and the two of them had a good visit.

Perhaps she'd try once again to convince the elderly woman to move to Texas with her. Granny could be stubborn on the subject, but Hallie hated the thought of her being in that little cabin all alone, away from a hospital or doctor. The closest clinic was less than thirty miles away, as the crow flew, but much farther by car over the winding back roads. Granny had a car but she wasn't that proficient a driver—and limited herself to buying her groceries at the small general store in Greens Hollow.

"Quit gabbin' with that man and get onto the business of springin' me," Granny called to Hallie from behind the bars.

Hallie glanced at Cam and thought she saw him hide a quick grin, but she couldn't be sure. Did he get a kick out of the old woman? Or did he want to get home? Just then the thought occurred to Hallie that he might have a wife waiting for him at that home, not to mention a houseful of little ones.

Then she thought again. The man didn't look like the type who *wanted* a wife. He had an attitude, and it wasn't one that rang with domesticity.

Hallie didn't have time to consider Cam further. He was studying her curiously—and she didn't want him to know she'd been thinking about him. Granny. Granny Pearl was the reason she was here in Greens Hollow—the only reason.

And she'd do well to remember that.

"About my grandmother," she said. "I demand you spring...uh, *release* her. She's elderly and shouldn't be spending even one night in jail."

"Not that easy, Ms. Cates. Your granny's been accused of a crime. There'll need to be a hearing—"

"A...hearing." Of course. That would clear her grandmother, she was sure. "How soon?" she asked cautiously.

"Five weeks from today—at the county seat. Judge McBain."

"*Five weeks!* Certainly you don't mean to keep her locked up until...? I mean, what about bail? Releasing her on her own recognizance?" Hallie didn't know much about legalities—but there was such a thing as *rights*.

"Believe me, I wouldn't want to keep that woman under lock and key any longer than I have to," he said. He leaned back in his desk chair, observing Granny Pearl for a moment over Hallie's left shoulder. "Tell you what," he said, righting the chair again. "I could be persuaded to release her into your custody until then—"

"Of course," Hallie answered without hesitation and rose from her seat as if that settled it.

"Ms. Cates, not so fast."

"I said I agreed."

He smiled slowly. "I was about to add, provided you accept full responsibility for your grandmother's actions, see she keeps to the straight and narrow, doesn't skip the country—"

Hallie gave an exasperated sigh. "Sheriff, this is all ridiculous. My grandmother is not a criminal. Of course, she'll obey the law."

"Right," he answered slowly. "And dogs don't hunt."

Her eyebrows shot up. "What's that supposed to mean?" she asked tersely.

"It means, dear Hallie, that you're gonna have your hands full with Ma Barker over there." He hooked a thumb in Granny's direction.

At the moment the woman looked positively angelic. Hallie shoved the jail keys across the desk at him. "Just open up, Sheriff, so I can take my grandmother home."

Chapter Two

Granny prattled on all the way to her cabin, not giving Hallie an inch of an opening, not a single chance to ask the big question: innocent or guilty? But for tonight Hallie wasn't sure she wanted an answer from the woman. She was tired from her long drive here, cranky from dealing with Cam Osborne and with Granny, and she wanted nothing more than to collapse into Granny's spare feather bed, snuggle into the sheets line-dried in the Arkansas sunshine and let sleep take her.

Tomorrow, or the day after, would be soon enough to tackle the truth—if Granny Pearl would give it to her—and to seek legal counsel for her.

Hallie could just picture the little old lady in court, cussing out the judge, the hunk of a man who arrested her, and the world in general. It would not be a pretty sight—and one Hallie hoped they wouldn't have to face.

George and Myrtle met them at the gate as Hallie turned her unflagging little Subaru into the drive. She saw why Granny was so devoted to the pair. They were cute, with their little black faces, their curiosity-filled eyes and friendly, brayed greeting.

"Oh, my little children are hungry," Granny said and was struggling with the passenger door handle before Hallie had brought the car to a full stop.

The creatures could survive easily on the grass they kept close-cropped in Granny's yard, not to mention the goodies they "stole" from her trash barrel, Hallie knew. But Granny insisted on feeding them extras—like her special corn bread, or whatever it was she had for her own supper each evening.

The woman was out of the car and hurrying, as nimble-footed as her goats, toward the back door. While Hallie struggled with her luggage in the trunk, Granny was back with two metal tins piled high with what looked suspiciously like her wonderful home-made honey biscuits. Hallie's tummy rumbled and for a moment she was envious of the goats. What she wouldn't give for a couple of those biscuits, warm from that old oven of Granny's.

"I hope you saved one or two of those for the person who sprang you from jail," Hallie teased as she carried her suitcase toward the cabin.

"Oh, Hallie, you must be thinkin' I'm a silly old woman." She dropped the tins and affectionately admonished the goats to eat with manners, then raced toward her granddaughter. "I reckon you must be hungry as a bear after that trek of yours all the way from Texas. Come on in the kitchen, girl."

It was nearly eleven, but Granny put on a spread

anyway, every leftover in her small, antiquated refrigerator, plus the remainder of her honey biscuits, complete with her to-die-for raspberry jam.

Hallie knew if she was going to be eating Granny's cooking she'd have to increase her exercise proportionately. And first off would be a walk through the piney woods that surrounded Granny's property to search for that so-called still Cam Osborne claimed Granny was putting to use.

She just hoped she didn't find one.

By the time Hallie had the dishes washed, Granny sat dozing in her rocker. How innocent she looked lost in sleep, her white hair spiked here and there in disarray, as if she'd been dragging a worried hand through it. Her skin was a soft, well-earned fine pattern of wrinkles, the pale pink blush on her cheeks natural and demure.

In repose she hardly looked like a moonshining grandmother. She didn't look like a woman who would sink her teeth into a man's arm, either—but Hallie had seen the evidence below Cam's shirtsleeve.

"C'mon, Granny Pearl, let's get you into bed, pronto," Hallie said, stirring her gently.

Granny mumbled something incoherent, something that sounded like…wh' lightnin'—which Hallie didn't exactly find reassuring.

In the morning she would definitely have to have that look around Granny's place—every square inch of it.

Cam didn't have a clue how he happened to find himself on the road to Pearl Cates's small cabin, but damned if that wasn't where his four-by-four was headed.

If he were wise he'd breeze right on past the old woman's property, maybe find that favorite stream of his, dig out the fishing rod he always carried with him, sit on the bank and sink a line—then spend the remainder of his afternoon forgetting Granny Pearl's redheaded granddaughter. And what she'd done to his usually peaceful night's slumber.

So she had glorious high cheekbones that glowed with the warm blush of summer, a pert little mouth—with that sassy tone not unlike her granny's—and green eyes a man could drown in if he were so inclined.

But Cam wasn't inclined.

He didn't intend to make room for a woman in his life ever again. When a smart man got burned, he didn't get near the flame a second time—and Cam considered himself a smart man.

He was only checking up on Pearl, he told himself, as he took the right fork toward her cabin in the woods. It was just a professional visit to be sure the old gal was keeping to the straight and narrow. And away from that still of hers.

Hallie was a bright woman, but he suspected she could be blinded by love—and she loved Granny Pearl. All of Greens Hollow did. Cam knew just how popular he'd be when the folks around here learned he'd brought the little old lady in and charged her with selling local lightning—especially when it cut off the supply for some of the town's denizens.

He doubted Granny Pearl would admit the truth to her granddaughter. On the contrary, she'd have Hallie believing Cam was the meanest man in the county, a man who picked on little old ladies, kicked dogs and dewinged butterflies.

Was that his reason for stopping by the Cates place? Was he afraid Granny would paint a villainous picture of him to Hallie?

Why should he care if Hallie thought him a louse, a blackguard? He *didn't* care. It was his job to uphold the law—and that's all he was doing.

He turned the black Cherokee into the gravel drive and caught himself searching around for Hallie. But he found only George and Myrtle, those two silly creatures who butted any man who came onto Granny's property or meant the old girl harm.

They didn't much like Cam. In fact, last time he was here they'd tried their best to render him a soprano for the rest of his days. Cam had had to be plenty fast on his feet to save his manhood and other much-needed body parts.

He was just wondering if there was any chance of winning the two critters over when he glanced up and saw Hallie coming out the front door of the cabin. His breath caught in his throat. The afternoon sun cutting through the trees caught the red in her hair, releasing its fire. Was her passion as fire-hot? Damned if he didn't wish he could sample it—just once.

"What brings you out here, Sheriff?" Her green eyes sparked with cool ice. "Searching for more little old ladies to arrest, are you?"

Her words hurt, but Cam wasn't about to admit it, even to himself. "Are you going to shoot me on the spot or may I come in?" He indicated the gate that stood between them, the watch goats protecting it. Protecting *her* from the likes of him.

She seemed to consider her options, and taking her sweet time to do it, too. "That all depends," she said finally, crossing her arms and eyeing him cautiously.

"On what?"

"On whether or not this is an...official visit."

Why did he have the feeling that whichever way he answered he was in trouble? If he said "official" she'd have her dander up royally, and if he said "friendly", well, let's just say, she didn't exactly look...friendly toward him at the moment.

"I just happened to be passing by," he parried. At least that was partly true. "I wanted to be sure Granny hadn't suffered any ill effects from her...time in jail."

That part Cam meant as well. He kind of liked the old woman, even if she was dangerous with those choppers of hers. As for her granddaughter...

Those blue jeans hugged her slender legs and shapely hips a little too delightfully for him to ignore at the moment. Her pert chin was raised a fractious notch, her mouth pursed like she'd just tasted an Arkansas persimmon—which only served to fire up his libido all the more. Her arms, crossed over her soft blouse, hid the shape of her breasts from view, but Cam had perfect recall from last night. Hallie Cates was missing nothing in the shape department.

Before Hallie could answer for her grandmother's health Granny appeared behind her on the porch. "What you awantin', Cam Osborne?" she barked in her unfriendliest voice.

"Good afternoon to you too, Granny Pearl," Cam said wryly, which seemed to take Granny aback for a moment.

"Don't go gettin' all smart-alecky with me, Sheriff," she said sharply. "I may be old, but I can still whup the likes of you."

Hallie hid a slow grin and cadged a peek at Cam. He'd enjoyed Granny's boast—and even looked like he might like to take the old girl on. That gave Hallie pause—Granny wouldn't win with the man.

No woman would, she suspected.

That sent a tingle of something skittering through her, something akin to...heat. Cam Osborne was a very good-looking man. She hadn't missed that fact last night, nor did she overlook it now. He stood as tall and rugged as a tree, his body every bit as hard, she suspected. The breeze feathered his dark hair, teasing it as a lover might. His face was all angles and planes, and every one of them pleasant to look at.

Granny had mentioned over breakfast this morning that the sheriff was single, that he'd come here from Chicago two years ago when Sheriff Potts had become ill and was forced to retire.

"And nothin' ain't been the same around here since," Granny had lamented.

Looking at Cam Osborne now, Hallie could believe he was a man who would change things. When he kissed a woman she'd stay kissed. He'd no doubt rattle her senses, as well as her good judgment.

"Hallie, you can stand here talking to this man all day if you want, but I got things that need doin'," Granny said and turned back toward the door. Hand on the screen she paused and glowered back at Cam. "You ain't come here on any more funny business, have you, Sheriff?"

"Funny business?" He raised an eyebrow.

"Like haulin' me back to that jail of yours."

"That all depends, Pearl. Have you been moonshining again?"

Granny wouldn't answer, just harumphed loudly and disappeared back inside the cabin.

Cam laughed low and long. Hallie added a glower of her own at the man, then reached for a quart fruit basket on the porch. "I have some raspberries to pick, so if you'll excuse me, Sheriff..." she said, leaving her sentence—and her meaning—hanging. Hallie didn't want Cam hanging around.

Instead Cam slipped open the latch on the gate. "I'm pretty good at berry picking," he said. "That is, if you don't mind some company."

She gave him a slow, evaluating glance. "Suit yourself," she said. "But...you'd better watch out for George and Myrtle."

If she'd hoped that word of caution would give him second thoughts about joining her, she'd been wrong. Cam snapped the gate closed behind him and made his way toward her, giving George and Myrtle a wide berth as he did so.

She had to grin at his wariness. It was nice to know the big, tough sheriff possessed a little fear at times.

"Where are these berry bushes?" he asked, falling into step beside her.

"Not far."

She kept moving, all too aware of him beside her.

He had that clean, fresh scent of a man, a mixture of soap and after-shave, and at the moment it was having a decided effect on her. His long legs could cover the terrain far quicker than she could, but he adjusted his stride to match hers. He moved with an easy grace, all-male and self-assured. There was a power to him that made her feel…vulnerable. And it was not a feeling she liked.

She didn't need to go losing her head over Cam Osborne or *any* man, especially one from Greens Hollow again. She'd learned that lesson one summer long ago. And she hadn't forgotten it.

Maybe it was why she didn't come back here to visit as often as she should. Or maybe it was just that her life in Fort Worth was so full, so busy. It was where she'd gone to heal, and for the most part, she had—except for that one tiny part of her she knew never could.

Hallie bit her lip and pushed away the memory. It was just coming back to Greens Hollow again that tugged the past into awareness—but as soon as she had everything with Granny and the sheriff settled, she could leave.

She only wished she could convince Granny Pearl to leave as well, to move in with her, where she could keep a close eye on her.

The bushes were over the next rise, a tangle of briars and sweet berries that could make her mouth water. Granny didn't prune them, just let them grow helter-skelter, wild as nature allowed. Hallie could already taste Granny's raspberry cobbler, her famous pancake syrup.

No one could match Granny's recipes, maybe because the prime ingredient was love. Hallie felt it, had always felt it, no matter how irascible the old girl could be at times.

"I hope you don't mind a few scratches on your hands," she said, "but it's the only way to pick."

"Hey, don't worry about me. I can endure a scratch or two."

"Even if you don't get to sample the bounty later?"

Cam grinned slowly. "Who says I won't?"

"I doubt very much that Granny'll invite you to supper—not after you carted her off to the clink yesterday." She frowned up at him. "Which brings up a question, Cam Osborne. Just what makes you so certain that Granny is operating a still? Have you actually *found* one?"

Hallie was certain he hadn't; this morning she'd had a thorough look around Granny's property, every nook and cranny of it. She'd found nothing.

"I wouldn't have brought the old gal in, if I hadn't," he answered.

Hallie gaped up at him for a long moment, then turned and plucked a berry. "I don't believe you," she said, absently dropping the berry into her container.

Had she somehow missed the site?

Hallie didn't think so.

"Would you like me to show it to you?" He picked a few raspberries from the vine, then leaned close to drop them into her basket.

He smelled like the mountain air, all clean and a little...untamed. And he rattled her, not just his claim about a still, but his presence so close to her.

She could see the fine lines that fanned out from his eyes, lines that said he'd lived with a few hurts in his life too—and for a moment Hallie wondered what they had been.

His eyes were dark, a deep brown that could fire with passion, but also bespoke an innate honesty. It was the honesty that had her worried, but the passion she was all too aware of, a passion she'd be a fool to fall susceptible to. And she wouldn't.

She turned back to her task. "I may just take you up on that, Sheriff," she said quietly, "but first I have raspberries to pick. Granny's expecting them."

"Fine by me."

Cam knew the woman beside him didn't believe him, and he wasn't eager to prove her wrong, to shatter that unshakable belief she had in Granny Pearl. Obviously Granny had not seen fit to fill her granddaughter in about her little…sideline. It might have made things easier for Cam if she had. Still, either way, he had the feeling Hallie was not about to warm to him anytime soon.

That shouldn't bother him, but for some reason— one he didn't want to think about too closely—it did. He reached into the brambles to pick, leaving the more accessible berries for Hallie. Not that she would probably appreciate his chivalry.

She worked busily, gathering her bounty, the sun gently bronzing her arms left bare by her sleeveless white blouse. It was open at the neck three buttons, revealing a tantalizing glimpse of skin. Every now and then she swiped at a bead of perspiration that trickled down her neck.

The sun was hot—and growing hotter.

"So tell me about Fort Worth. What do you do there?" Cam was certain talk was better than fantasizing about whether she'd catch the latest bead of perspiration traveling toward that delectable hollow between her breasts.

She glanced up, her green eyes showing surprise that he'd ask a question about her personally. Well, damn, did she doubt he could be interested in one beautiful woman? He shouldn't be, but he was curious about Hallie Cates.

She plucked another raspberry. "I'm a teacher, elementary school."

"A teacher?" Cam gave a slow smile. "You don't look like a schoolteacher to me."

She raised her head again. "And just what in your estimation does a schoolteacher look like?" she asked.

"They wear their hair in tight little buns and have crow's feet," he answered. "At least they did when I was a kid."

She let a smile slip at his remark, just a small one. "Give me a few years," she returned. "Second-graders can age you rapidly."

He liked her smile, wanted to see more of it, wondered what it would take to shake her dislike of him. Short of forgetting all about that still Pearl had been putting to considerable use. "Is that what grade you teach—second?"

She nodded.

He touched a red springy curl that whispered across the fair skin at her temple. "You, pretty lady, don't have anything to worry about in the age department. And I'd wager all the little boys have a crush on you.'' He knew *he* would if he were in that classroom.

A small laugh bubbled up from her throat. "A few," she answered.

"I thought so. And how about *big* boys—any...men in your life, Hallie Cates?"

Why was he waiting for her answer? Why should he care if there was one—or twenty-one? But it seemed he was curious.

"That, Sheriff, is getting nosy—but since you asked, *no*. Teaching keeps me busy."

"What a shame."

"What...?"

That hadn't been meant for Hallie's ears. "I, uh, was just wondering how many berries we need," he answered quickly.

She gave him a long, scrutinizing glance. "Right," she said.

When she finally allowed that they'd picked enough to satisfy Granny's recipe, Cam took the basket. "Let's go take a look at Granny's little enterprise," he said. "It's just at the end of that hollow."

Hallie gaped. "That close to the cabin? I thought stills were always well hidden."

"What can I say, the old girl obviously wasn't worried about getting caught."

By the sheriff, Hallie thought. She couldn't imagine what it was the man planned to show her. She'd seen nothing that even vaguely resembled a still hidden anywhere on Granny's property.

But Granny was just foxy enough to be up to something—and Cam seemed entirely too confident.

Chapter Three

It was cooler here in the hollow. The afternoon breeze whispered through, ruffling the ends of Hallie's hair, the thick strands of Cam's. The air was redolent with dogwood and a hint of pine. From above, the birds chattered away noisily.

"So just where *is* this so-called still you uncovered?" Hallie asked as Cam did his best imitation of a man searching around for a favorite pair of boots, and coming up empty.

Unless the still was small enough to hide under a rock it wasn't anywhere around—and Hallie began to feel a whole lot better. She didn't know whether Granny Pearl was innocent of Cam's charges or up to her eyeballs in mischief, but she sincerely hoped the former was true and not the latter.

Cam let loose with a colorful curse even Granny could appreciate.

Hallie smiled. "Maybe this isn't the right hollow.

Maybe it's somewhere else and your memory is a teensy bit off.'' Her reply was meant more to antagonize than any real offer of explanation—and it hit the mark.

Cam's eyes blazed. "Oh, no. This is the right spot all right. That sneaky old biddy has moved it, that's what. She had no intention of shutting down operations. She's just gone underground."

"Underground?"

"A figure of speech. These things can be mighty portable in this part of the country. But I didn't think Pearl had it in her to up and transport—" He stopped short and spun around to gaze dangerously at Hallie. "Unless maybe…"

"Maybe what?"

"*You* helped the old girl."

"*Me?*" Hallie squeaked with indignation…and surprise.

"Oh, yeah—*you,* and Granny Pearl." His eyes narrowed. "Last night. Or maybe this morning—before sunup."

"I had nothing to do with hiding anything, Sheriff. And I'm not a hundred percent convinced there ever was a still. After all, I only have your say-so on that, now don't I?"

Cam rubbed his jaw for a long moment. "Okay—so maybe I'm jumping the gun a bit here. After all, I don't have proof you were involved…" The glint in his dark eyes suggested that if he found out she was, there was going to be hell to pay.

The sick feeling she'd had a short time before returned. She'd have to question Granny, have to get some sort of answer out of her. If Granny was, indeed, moonshining...

Just then Cam's beeper went off. "Damn!" he said. "I gotta get back to the Jeep. But this isn't finished, Hallie Cates."

She followed him back through the hollow. His stride was long, eating up ground as he went. The breeze all but disappeared as they entered Granny's enclosed yard, the air turning hot and still. Hallie swatted at a fly that buzzed around, and hurried to keep pace with Cam.

When he reached the Cherokee he leaned inside and used the radio. Hallie heard the static but not the words, heard Cam's terse reply. "I'll be right there," he said to whoever was on the other end.

He had bigger fish to fry than Granny at the moment, it seemed. Perpetrators more frightening than little old ladies who might, or might not, be dabbling in moonshine. For a moment she was worried for Cam. Being sheriff around these parts had to carry a certain element of risk, of danger, she was sure.

However, she suspected Cam Osborne could take care of himself. His size more than proved that. Just his bark would scare the criminally bent into running for cover. It was only Granny who refused to be intimidated by the big tough man.

"I've got some trouble in town to deal with," he said as he put the Jeep into gear, "but I'll be back."

"Is that a threat or a promise, Sheriff?" Her words were spoken with more bravado than she felt on the inside.

He didn't answer, just turned his attention to backing out of Granny's drive, then disappeared up the road, leaving a trail of dust in his wake.

"You should learn to respect your elders, missy. Am I makin' moonshine and sellin' it to half the county like Cam Osborne says? How can you ask such a thing?"

"I am asking—and you are going to answer me," Hallie said, intending to wring the truth from Granny Pearl if it was the last thing she did.

And preferably before the sheriff came back.

Granny rinsed the raspberries Hallie and Cam had picked. A plump young chicken stewed on the stove, while Hallie prepared a salad of greens from the garden.

"An answer, Granny," she repeated when the old woman clamped her mouth into a thin stubborn line. "Did Cam find a still on this property?"

Granny raised her chin. "Says he did."

"I *know* what he said. Is it true?"

"Maybe 'tiz, maybe 'taint." Granny stirred the rich berries into the cobbler, popped the pan into her relic of an oven and wiped her hands on her apron as if she were done with the conversation, as well as the cobbler.

The woman could be exasperating to say the least.

"You're not going to answer me, are you?" Hallie said, finishing with the salad. She set the bowl on the small dining table, then turned and glowered at her kitchen companion.

"What was the question?"

What indeed. Granny could fake a sudden case of forgetfulness faster than anyone Hallie knew. "So

that's the way you're going to play this. Okay..."
She raised her hands in a show of defeat. "If you
won't talk to me, you can just talk to the sheriff
when he returns."

Granny snorted. "That man's comin' back here?
What fer?"

Maybe to haul Granny back to his iron-barred hotel, Hallie thought dismally. Butting heads with this
cantankerous woman was not the way she'd intended
to spend her vacation. Neither was dealing with one
equally determined sheriff. "He's coming back here
to talk to you—and he won't be half as patient in
getting his answers," she warned.

At the moment she wouldn't blame the man if he
brought along thumbscrews to use on the old girl.

Supper was eaten in testy silence, neither woman
ready to give an inch in their cold war. Hallie wondered just how much patience Cam would have with
Granny. She got the feeling he was a strictly by-the-
book kind of sheriff. Do the crime and you do the
time. That would be Cam. Even if the offender was
a little old lady.

He'd come from Chicago, with its big-city problems. And somewhere in that big city he'd decided
it was safer not to be too trusting—of anyone. Life
had made him wary.

Perhaps because life had done the same for Hallie,
she could recognize it.

But she didn't want to doubt Granny Pearl. Her
grandmother was the one she'd always believed in,
the one who had always loved her, *would* always
love her.

Hallie washed up the last of the supper dishes and

tried not to think about the man who would be returning here tonight. Cam Osborne made her nervous—and not just because of Granny Pearl. He made her nervous on some feminine level. He was just too good-looking, too...*male* for a woman's own good.

She rubbed her temples. A headache had begun to throb. But she wasn't sure she could blame that entirely on Cam. Granny Pearl had every bit as much to do with her present state of anxiety.

The disturbance in town proved to be minor. Two high school kids fighting over a girl. Cam had separated the boys, given them a strong talking-to, then called their respective parents to take them home.

The girl they were feuding over was a pretty one. Nearly as pretty as Hallie Cates, he thought, comparing. How could he blame the two for going head-to-head over a good-looking female? Hell, he'd probably do the same.

Over Hallie?

Yeah, over Hallie, he admitted with grim reluctance.

When had his hormones taken this turn? he wanted to know.

When he'd first laid eyes on the woman, that's when.

Cam let out a solitary oath as his Jeep raced along the dusty back roads. He had no business thinking of Hallie in any regard except as Pearl's granddaughter, *Pearl's granddaughter who would soon be returning to Fort Worth.*

If there was one thing Cam had learned back in

Chicago it was to keep a safe distance from the gentler sex. Gentler? He scoffed. Elise had been far from "gentler" as it turned out. His former wife had taken him for one helluva ride—and Cam had no intention of ever getting on *that* train again.

If he were wise he'd get this interrogation of Pearl over with—and fast—then get on back to town. Maybe he could find a poker game, drink a few beers, and hope that when he fell asleep he didn't dream of one fiery-tempered redhead.

He saw Hallie and Granny Pearl sitting on the porch enjoying the cool evening air when he pulled into the drive. Granny Pearl lit out as soon as she spotted him, taking off through the yard, no doubt with the trumped-up notion of communing with those goats of hers.

The old girl was going to be contrary—but then, Cam hadn't expected anything else.

He waved to Hallie and unlatched the gate.

"Hello, Cam," she said as he neared the porch.

His libido bucked just hearing his name roll off that pretty tongue of hers. Her hair was tucked up and held in place with a tortoiseshell comb of sorts, but small, wispy tendrils escaped here and there and teased at the blush on her cheeks.

She'd changed into a pair of white shorts that made her legs look a good mile longer than they already were, and all too shapely for his peace of mind. The top she wore was a pretty shade of mint— and made her green eyes look big and wide in the evening twilight. If he'd ever wanted to touch a woman, it was this woman…at this moment.

He jammed his hands deep into his pockets where

they wouldn't be tempted to follow any wayward path. "Mind if I join you?" he asked, indicating the wicker porch chair Granny had vacated. "It looks as if I might have to wait the old girl out."

"Be my guest, but it may be a long wait. Granny, uh, doesn't want to talk to you."

Cam let a half smile curl at the edge of his mouth. "Yeah, well, she's going to have to sometime."

Hallie tucked one leg up under her and turned toward Cam. "I tried to get something out of her myself after you left, but I didn't have much luck, I'm afraid. You're not going to threaten her with jail again, are you?"

Cam gave her a long, considering glance. In addition to the defiant set of her chin there was an edge of worry to her demeanor. Hallie cared about Granny Pearl.

He tunneled his fingers through his hair and studied the deepening shadows in the yard, wishing Pearl would come clean—and give up this moonshine nonsense, save *him* a whole lot of headaches. "You got any better suggestions?"

Hallie didn't, short of the thumbscrews she'd considered earlier. With the firm jut of Cam's jaw she didn't think she should suggest any such possibility. He looked just perturbed enough with Granny to go for it.

Tonight, as before, he was dressed casually, this time in jeans and a white, polo-style shirt that contrasted with his outdoorsy tan. No uniform. Probably saved them for hauling in the tough guys, *real* fugitives, she thought. With Granny it was the "folksy" approach—not that Hallie suspected it would gain him anything with the old girl. When Granny made up her mind not to talk, she wouldn't talk.

"Well, if you're determined to wait her out, how about a dish of cobbler? It *could* be a long night, Sheriff."

"With raspberries?" His mood quickly brightened. Enormously. Suddenly he didn't seem to mind how long the little standoff took.

"With raspberries," she admitted.

Hallie just wished she didn't feel so much like a traitor offering Granny's lovely dessert to the other side. Granny herself had been about to indulge before Cam drove up. Now she was out there in her big yard somewhere, swallowed up by the darkness. But then—that was her choice. She could have stuck around and answered Cam's questions like a sane, sensible woman. Instead she'd left Hallie to deal with the man.

How could Granny have gotten herself—and Hallie—into such a plight?

"I'll go get that cobbler. Don't go anywhere," she quipped, as if Cam had the slightest intention of moving off the porch anytime tonight.

"I'll be here when you get back," he answered with a low chuckle.

Hallie swallowed a groan. Didn't he have anyone from the Most Wanted list to apprehend? She disappeared inside, letting the door bang behind her.

Cam watched her go—enjoying that enticing little wiggle to her hips—before settling back in the porch chair to relax. This job was beginning to offer a few rewards. He could sit back, look up at the emerging stars and let his suspect come to him. He even had one pretty woman to keep him company while he waited.

There was a problem or two, however, with his scenario.

Granny wouldn't voluntarily come out of hiding—and he didn't relish bucking George and Myrtle to go and get her. Also, he found Hallie far too tempting for his own good.

Everything about the woman told him he'd better hold onto his good sense. He didn't need to go off the deep end over some female, not when he was finally beginning to find himself again, to sort through his anger—and his mistrust—and get on with life, such as it was.

So, why was he waiting for Hallie to come banging through that screen door? He didn't think it was just anticipation of the cobbler, no matter how tasty it might be. Oh, no, the woman could rein him in if he wasn't careful. Damned careful.

Hallie returned, carrying a tray with three bowls of Granny's dessert piled high with the berries they'd picked that afternoon.

"Three? You must have high hopes your grandmother will see reason and hustle herself back up here to the porch," Cam said, helping her with the tray. Their fingers brushed as he took it from her and Cam saw a bolt of awareness in her green eyes.

So, he affected her, he thought. That was only half what her touch did to him.

Damn, what was it about the woman?

He settled the tray on a nearby table, hoping his own reaction wasn't equally revealing. She drew away and wrapped her arms around herself as if she were cold. Or…warding off danger.

"I'm hoping Granny will see reason," she said softly. "Or that the dessert will lure her back."

The dessert had lured *him* all right. Or rather, Hallie had. He wondered if it was too late to get in on that poker game back in town. If he stuck around here he might just end up with more trouble than he bargained for.

And not from Granny Pearl.

Hallie picked up one of the desserts for herself and retreated to the porch railing to sit and stare out into the night. Okay, she admitted it, Cam set her pulses to racing. And being alone with him in the darkening night wasn't helping the situation. The touch of their hands had been inadvertent, but not without reaction. At least on her part.

This wasn't like her. "Tell me about Chicago," she said after sampling a small bite of Granny's cobbler.

Cam had seated himself near her on the porch railing, but at the simple question he stood up and set his bowl back on the tray, then paced to the end of the porch. "What about it?" he asked.

"Were you a cop there?"

Hallie meant to make conversation, but she had to admit to a certain…curiosity about the man. She wanted to know more about him than what Granny had told her.

"Yeah, I was a cop."

"Job burnout?"

He glanced back at her. "What?"

"The reason you left—job burnout? I mean, why did you come here? To Greens Hollow?"

He dragged a hand through his hair. "I was offered the job. I took it. Any other questions?"

She'd gotten more information out of Granny Pearl than she had from Cam. He'd clammed up like a day lily. "I was just curious why someone would leave a big city—with all its advantages—to come to this place—which has few."

"Maybe I'm not into...*advantages,*" he said sharply.

He could have been—like his partner. He could have lined his pockets well. He still couldn't believe the payoffs Lazaro had been taking, payoffs to look the other way. Lazaro had looked the other way when that last drug deal went down—and it had nearly gotten Cam killed.

There was a bond between a cop and his fellow cop, at least that was what Cam had foolishly believed back then. His partner had shattered the myth.

A few months later Elise shattered a few other myths Cam had erroneously held. He hadn't cared to stick around to see what else life had to offer.

As far as Cam was concerned, the conversation was over. Hallie Cates was too damned inquisitive for a man with wounds that were not quite fully healed.

He should go off in search of Pearl. That, after all, was why he was here, to interrogate the old gal. But at the moment Hallie's wide, lustrous eyes, and equally lustrous lips temporarily derailed those intentions. She was all he could think about.

His pacing had brought him within an inch of her.

She smelled of sweetness and moonlight. He took her dessert and set it aside, then drew her up from the porch rail and into his arms. He wanted only to taste that mouth of hers, one little kiss, a sampling of what he didn't need from her—and shouldn't take. He'd caught her off guard—and he supposed he should feel guilty about that. But he couldn't seem to summon up the appropriate remorse.

Not now. Maybe later.

She felt just too damned good in his arms, her lips too tempting.

Sexy. The man kissed so sexy that Hallie felt herself pulled into the maelstrom that was Cam. She hadn't had time to think, to react, before she was taking everything he had to offer. His mouth on hers was possessive, his hold on her gripping, relentless.

She reveled in the taste of him, the sensual movement of his mouth on hers.

If she'd ever been kissed like this she didn't remember it. And a kiss like this she didn't think she could ever have forgotten.

Nor would she forget this one.

His hands tangled in her hair. The small comb she'd clipped into her hairstyle fell with a clatter to the porch and Hallie only vaguely heard it. All she knew was that Cam was devouring her common sense, that little niggling voice that said she should pull away, end this before she no longer could. And she would—in just a moment.

She only wanted one more taste of the man, one more crush of his body to hers, hard, demanding, powerful, before she returned to the reality of the situation.

"Cam Osborne, just what in tarnation are you doing with my granddaughter?"

inveigled along to assist us in our quest. At the moment, she is busy—

"Cut it out. Just what in thunder are you up to, you old scoundrel?"

Chapter Four

Cam wasn't sure whether to be annoyed or grateful for the surprise interruption of the most enjoyable kiss he'd ever experienced in all his born days. Granny Pearl's sense of timing left a lot to be desired, there was no doubt about that. But the old woman could be a hellcat—he'd learned that when he'd confiscated her whiskey and herded her into the jailhouse yesterday afternoon.

He broke loose from Hallie with a jolt and tried to assume a look of choirboy innocence—but it wasn't working on Pearl. Not in the least. She had blood in her eye, and if that wasn't warning enough, she snatched up her rusty old shotgun from its hiding place under the porch and aimed it dead center, Cam swore, at one tender part of his anatomy.

He didn't know if that bazooka of hers was capable of firing or not, but he was taking no chances. He took an additional step away from Hallie, the woman who'd just turned him inside out with one sweet tasty kiss, and faced down the old one who threatened a less pleasant form of body rearrangement.

"Pearl," he said, his voice sounding a little huskier than usual. He didn't like the barrel of a gun pointed anywhere in his direction. If the old gal was the shot he feared she was, his life could be permanently altered. "Put down the gun like a nice girl and have a dish of cobbler—then we'll, uh, talk."

"We'll talk right now, Cam Osborne—and with this here gun for inspiration. Just what do you mean kissin' my Hallie?"

Cam knew he couldn't let the old woman get the better of him. "Kissing? Why, Pearl, honey, that was just a friendly peck."

"Friendly?" She leveled the gun for dead aim. "I don't want you gettin' anything *close* to friendly with the likes of us," she sang out in that cranky voice of hers he was all too familiar with of late. "And I know kissin' when I see it. I might be old, Cam Osborne, but I ain't no fool—so don't you go takin' me for one."

"Granny, please, put down that gun right now," Hallie warned from somewhere beside him. "Cam...Cam didn't mean anything by that kiss."

The hell he didn't—but now, he was sure, was not the time to argue that point. "That's right, Pearl, it was totally innocent. Didn't mean a thing." He flashed Hallie a smile that said otherwise, then returned his gaze to Pearl.

The smile hadn't gotten past her. Damn, but the woman had eyes as sharp as a crow's. "I seen that,

Sheriff," she said. The gun barrel began to wave in front of him. "Don't make me blast you one."

Pearl was none too steady. One false move and it could be curtains for him. "Wouldn't dream of it, Pearl. Now, please put down the gun."

If she didn't, he was through dealing with her. He'd have to tackle her around the knees and hope for the best. Why hadn't he stayed in Chicago where the natives weren't half this unfriendly?

He took a step closer, then another.

Pearl didn't retreat as he'd hoped, just stabbed the gun toward him.

"Granny!"

Before Cam knew what had happened Hallie flew past him and grabbed at the antiquated weapon. The damn thing went off in a cloud of dark smoke and smelly powder. The bullet had to have been in the barrel for forty years, give or take ten.

Cam let out a whoosh of breath when he realized Hallie was fine—and so was Pearl.

He was still standing, too.

He wrenched the gun away from the pair, then glowered at Hallie. "That was a fool thing to do. You could have gotten yourself shot," he barked at her, sounding sharper than he'd intended. But just the thought of what could have happened to her made the blood chill in his veins.

"Well, pardon me for rescuing you, Sheriff," she said snippily. "Next time I'll let Granny blow you to kingdom come."

That would be preferable to seeing Hallie hurt, Cam decided, not over his pique at the two Cates women. "Pearl wouldn't have shot me," he said more confidently than he felt on the inside. "Isn't that right, Pearl?"

"Don't you go takin' any bets on that, Sheriff," Granny returned. "And you'd better keep yourself away from my granddaughter—or you'll have *me* to answer to."

And that old shotgun of hers, no doubt, Cam was certain.

But Pearl was right about one thing. If he knew what was good for him he'd put a healthy distance between Hallie and himself.

And not just because of any threats of Granny Pearl's.

Cam faced the old girl. "Okay, Pearl—no more kissing. Scout's honor," he agreed reluctantly—but sensibly.

He couldn't look at Hallie, couldn't let himself even think of the succulence of that tempting mouth of hers—or all would be lost. He'd withdraw his promise faster than a skunk crossing the road.

"No more hangin' around her neither, Cam Osborne," she added, not satisfied until she had him in a vise she could squeeze until he begged for mercy.

"Unless it's business," Cam affirmed. "We have a few things left unsettled, Pearl."

Granny snorted indelicately. "Says you." She started toward the back door. "You comin', Hallie? This man needs to go home," she said in firm dismissal. "We don't need the likes of him hangin' around where he ain't wanted."

Hallie knew she should follow after her grandmother. She also knew she owed Cam an apology for Granny's behavior. She'd involved herself in that kiss of his—and for that he'd found himself at the business end of Granny's old gun.

Cam didn't deserve that.

"I don't think she's in any mood to be civil tonight," she told Cam, knowing *that* was an understatement. "Just give me some time with her. I promise I'll talk to her, get some answers out of her about the still. *And* if she's involved." Hallie sincerely hoped Granny wasn't. But things didn't look favorable. She glanced down at the weapon Cam had confiscated from her grandmother. "I—I'm sorry about the gun," she added.

What would she do if Cam wanted to press charges for tonight's little fiasco? Had Granny even thought of that? Or about how much she'd frightened them all?

"This isn't finished, Hallie, not by a long shot." Cam wasn't sure whether he was referring to his attraction to her or the situation with Granny, he only knew the moonlight glinting in her velvet-green eyes at the moment had his mind in a muddle.

"I think it's best we leave everything be for tonight," she commented. "I—I'll take charge of the weapon, see she doesn't get her hands on it."

She reached for the gun, but Cam held it aloft. "This thing is dangerous. I don't want it in Pearl's hands." He took a step away from Hallie and checked the barrel to be certain there wasn't another bullet lurking inside. Satisfied it was empty he snapped it shut again. "Does the old girl have any more ammo for this blunderbuss?" he asked.

"I doubt it—at least, I don't think so."

"All the same, I'm keeping it under lock and key. No offense, Hallie."

She planted her hands on her trim, pretty hips. "I'm quite capable of looking after Granny Pearl— and the gun," she said with just the right smattering of indignation in her dulcet tone.

"I'm not entirely sure of that, Hallie Cates. It seems your grandmother keeps getting herself in deeper and deeper."

And maybe Cam was doing the same. With Hallie. No maybe about it.

He'd made a promise to Pearl to keep his hands off her tempting granddaughter—and that was a promise he definitely needed to keep.

When Hallie entered the cabin Granny was pacing in agitation. And Hallie knew that innocent kiss with Cam was the cause. Or maybe the kiss wasn't so innocent after all.

Hallie's lips still sang from the feel of it. Her heart still beat a little too fast.

"Granny, maybe you'd better sit down." She motioned to the well-worn rocker across the room.

Granny didn't move, just narrowed her shrewd gaze on Hallie. "I don't need to be asittin' in my rocker," she returned.

Her tone was testy, but beneath it Hallie sensed the worry.

Worry for Hallie.

"Okay, Granny, let's talk about it," she said. She knew Granny didn't exactly like the sheriff, much less Hallie kissing him, but she had the feeling there was more to it than that.

There were a few extra unwarranted wrinkles in that frown of hers.

The old woman resumed her pacing, her usually indomitable mouth silent for a long moment—as if now that she finally had Hallie's attention, she didn't know how to proceed.

Hallie went to her, and noticed the faint mist of tears in her eyes, tears that if Hallie mentioned, Granny would firmly deny. "Granny, that kiss with Cam didn't mean anything, just like Cam said. And I'm saying it, too."

Hallie didn't like to see Granny like this.

"I certainly hope so, Hallie, but you wasn't exactly kissin' like it didn't mean anything."

Hallie's cheeks grew warm.

Granny drew away and paced over to her rocker, after all, and sat down. The chair began to hum on the old floorboards. Granny was agitated.

"It's just that I don't want to see you losin' your head over someone from these parts, Hallie. I don't want to see you get hurt like before."

Like before. Hallie drew in a ragged breath. So that was what had Granny all in a tizzy. That summer she'd thought she was in love with Tommy Lamont. That summer Hallie *had* gotten hurt. Here in Greens Hollow. The summer Hallie had been foolishly in love, or what she'd thought was love, with Tommy Lamont.

It was why she didn't come back here as often as she should to see Granny. The town reminded her of too much, her pain that never quite left her.

That summer just before her eighteenth birthday she'd gotten pregnant—not intentionally; she and

Tommy had had a lot of growing up to do. Tommy, more than she, as it turned out.

Tommy Lamont hadn't had the backbone to be a father, had wanted nothing to do with the baby. He'd been afraid of what his dad would say, what the town would say. The son of the town minister wasn't supposed to get in trouble.

Hallie couldn't deny his reaction had devastated her, but she'd wanted her baby, wanted it with every frightened bone in her body—but it wasn't to be.

"Don't think I don't know about the baby, Hallie—and the miscarriage. Losin' that child was the reason you was hurtin'—not 'cause of that louse Tommy Lamont."

Hallie squeezed her eyes shut. She'd been so lost in her own pain that summer she'd never considered Granny could be wise to the situation. "Why—why didn't you say something?"

She could have done with some warm hugs from Granny, that bony, old shoulder of hers to cry on.

"I reckoned you'd tell me in your own time, girl. Then you went back home. I knew from the heartbreak of your letters that you'd lost the baby. You didn't return for a few summers, and by then I didn't know how to bring it up."

Until now, Hallie thought. Until seeing her only granddaughter kissing another "louse" from Greens Hollow.

But Cam Osborne wasn't Tommy Lamont.

No, perhaps he was someone a little more risky.

Hallie was older, wiser now, but there was still a part of her that was vulnerable. That she didn't want to fool herself about.

"I'd'a torn that Lamont kid limb from limb for the hurt he caused you—but he left town and ain't been seen around here since," Granny added. "I s'pose it was good riddance though—even if it did deny me a little justice."

Hallie forced a smile to her lips. Granny would always be there for her, no matter what—had *always* been there. She knew that, but she loved to hear her grandmother say so—and so eloquently.

"Thank you for telling me," she said softly. "Thank you for being you." She hugged the old girl and got a big hug in return.

"Hallie, you're the only kin I got in this world. I'm an old woman—and an old woman worries."

Hallie smiled. "I know, Granny, but there's no need. I don't intend to lose my head, *or my heart,* to anyone, especially not some sheriff who goes around arresting little old ladies."

Granny gave her a piercing glance, studying her intently. Her words seemed to satisfy the old girl for the present. She moved to get out of her rocker. "I better get them cobbler dishes washed up now," she said, as if putting the conversation behind her.

"I'll do it, Granny," Hallie insisted.

Hallie needed something to do at the moment— and time to think about this turn of events.

Somehow last evening had derailed Hallie from her primary objective, her grandmother, and the trouble the woman had gotten herself into—not facing the past again, the hurtful, painful past. And definitely not thrilling to a kiss on a warm Arkansas evening with the town sheriff.

She intended to be single-minded from now on; she intended to get to the bottom of just what it was her grandmother was up to. She'd promised Cam Osborne, but she also needed to know for herself.

And for Granny's well-being.

Making moonshine was against the law, though it had once been a cottage industry in these hills, a part of the area's history. And Granny Pearl had no business dabbling in it.

Hallie slipped into her jeans, pulled on a big shirt she tied at the waist Daisy-Mae style, drew her hair up in a bouncy ponytail and headed out in search of "evidence," *anything* Cam might have on her grandmother.

The late morning sun felt good on her face, the dogwood bloomed in profusion and Hallie had a hard time believing all wasn't right in this part of Granny's world.

The ever-curious George and Myrtle trailed along behind, keeping close tabs on her as she poked in every clump of tall grass. She checked under every bush and beneath piles of abandoned trash. She searched a deep well and inside the rusted-out shell of a car that had been her grandfather's.

Hallie remembered him. He'd been a simple man, smelling gently of tobacco and Ben-Gay for his rheumatism—and she'd missed him terribly after his death when she was seven. Her father had died a few years later in a light plane crash. Both deaths had been very hard on Granny Pearl.

But the old girl was made of stern stuff. She possessed an inner strength Hallie had to admire.

An inner strength laced with perverse stubbornness—Hallie reconsidered.

But perhaps that stubbornness had gotten her through a lot.

With a struggle she tugged a pair of old tires out of a low ravine, searching for any signs of a still, even though she could tell the debris hadn't been disturbed in years. She jumped back with a startled yelp as some furry creature skittered away, squeaking with indignation at having his morning nap disturbed.

It was just a possum, she decided, feeling fortunate it hadn't been anything more ominous—like a snake.

A short while later she decided there was no still anywhere on the property, despite Cam's claims to the contrary. If Granny were indeed up to something illegal, there was not one shred of evidence of it around there.

She was determined to drag Granny to a lawyer, kicking and screaming if necessary, to fight these ridiculous charges. As far as she was concerned they were frivolous, and she wanted to get the matter settled once and for all.

"Come on, Myrtle, George. I've had enough of this nonsense." She ruffled their ears. "Next time that sheriff comes around here," she told them, "you have my permission to butt him to the other side of the county."

By the time she returned to the cabin she found Granny's old clunker of a car was missing. A note sat propped on the kitchen table, resting neatly against the sugar bowl. Gone quilting it read, and

Hallie knew her grandmother, and the other ladies of the town, were stitching and gossiping about everything that went on in these parts.

At least she wasn't off dabbling in moonshine, Hallie decided with a certain relief. Tomorrow she would happily report to Cam that she'd found nothing on Granny's property—no still, no evidence one had ever been there.

At last she had that settled.

Now if she could only forget the kiss she'd shared with him last night, the feel of his hands in her hair, the male scent of him with that hint of soap and fresh mountain air. Her heart still fluttered like a skittery bird in her chest, the dreams she'd had last night failing to dissipate with the cool light of day. When she tried to put him out of her mind, she found she couldn't.

Damn the man and his sensuality.

Maybe she'd bake a pie to take her mind off everything. Mmmm—a cherry pie baked with those fat, tart cherries Granny had picked from her trees last fall and industriously canned. She'd surprise Granny with it when she returned.

Dutifully she began to assemble the ingredients, cherries, sugar, flour—but then her scoop caught on something in the flour canister.

Hallie peered inside and drew out a white-dusted piece of paper, the spidery script definitely Granny's handwriting.

A forgotten recipe?

Hallie shook the flour dust off it and smoothed it out on the countertop, scanning it with her gaze. Then she scanned it again.

"Why that little weasel!"

It was a recipe all right—and it was for moonshine.

By the time Hallie's scalawag relative returned home later that evening Hallie was fit to be tied. Somehow she'd managed to finish the pie—it was baking nicely in Granny's archaic oven—but the excitement of surprising the old girl with it had definitely waned.

"Granny, we need to talk." Hallie fluttered the "recipe" in front of her. A few small particles of flour dust wafted softly to the floor, leaving no doubt as to where Hallie had found it.

The crafty old girl eyed the bits of falling flour, then the thin paper in Hallie's hand. She grabbed at it, but Hallie was quicker.

"Oh, no you don't, you little outlaw. I'm keeping this—and *you* are going to tell me how you've been putting it to use."

Not *if*, no more ifs—the old biddy was up to her neck in mischief and Hallie knew it. Oh, Lord, Cam had been right. Her grandmother was as guilty as sin.

"Tell me where you've hidden that still. I've searched every square inch of this property and couldn't find it. But I know it's here. You're not going to get away with this."

Granny set her worn pocketbook down on a nearby chair and absently poked a white hair back into her bun atop her head. "Hallie Cates, I don't know what in thunder you're talkin' about—and I'll thank you to give me back my recipe."

Hallie's eyes narrowed. "Aha! Then you admit it—it's *your* recipe!"

"Of course it's my recipe. Been in my family for generations. Now give it to me." She reached for the paper again.

"Not…on…your…life." Hallie lifted the paper higher. "Now, I suggest you talk. And fast."

"I don't know what about," Granny said innocently. She marched past Hallie toward the kitchen and the smells emanating from it.

"Granny!" Hallie called after her, her tone laced with annoyance, exasperation.

Granny ignored her.

"I see you've done something useful around here besides pokin' in my business." She popped open the oven and sniffed deeply. "Mm-mmm, cherry pie—my favorite," she said, then snapped the oven door closed. "Don't you go givin' none of it to that sheriff neither," she warned.

Hallie gave a groan. Her grandmother could change the subject faster than anyone she knew. The old girl wasn't about to spill the beans. Hallie knew her only too well. She could pull the old gal's fingernails out one by one and the ornery woman still wouldn't talk.

"Granny, I thought you asked me here to help you, but how can I help if you refuse to level with me?"

Granny's bright eyes snapped. "I asked you here to bounce me out of that hellhole that sheriff calls a jail."

And now that she had, Hallie was to just back off? Cam would certainly find that still before Hallie did, all the evidence he'd need to send Granny up the river, for sure.

Her voice was solemn. "Granny, I think we should see a lawyer." If Hallie couldn't convince her how much trouble she was in, perhaps an attorney could.

"A lawyer? What fer? I ain't never needed one of them fellas in my life, and I don't need one now."

Hallie decided this was not the time to point out there were just as many females among the lawyer ranks as "fellas." All Granny knew was Greens Hollow—and the way things used to be "in her day."

Hallie unfolded the recipe she had clutched in her hand and glanced down at it. A smoking gun? Not quite—but it definitely did not look good for Granny Pearl's innocence.

Hallie didn't know what she was going to do with Granny.

And she didn't know what she was going to tell Cam.

Chapter Five

By the next afternoon things were testy around the small cabin. Granny remained mum on the subject of her recent escapades, and Hallie couldn't budge another word out of her.

She needed air and a little space, a little perspective. She made a shopping list and decided to go into town for supplies. She left Granny behind, puttering around the yard, tending her two precious goats and replanting the flower bulbs they'd dug up—*again*. Hallie only hoped Granny didn't have that alleged still planted somewhere in that backyard, as well.

But she didn't want to think about that today, nor about what she should report to Cam. She hadn't yet decided to tell him about her find in the flour canister. It was far too incriminating for Granny.

Granny wasn't taking a whit of this seriously— except for her feud with Cam. And her granddaughter's kissing him.

Perhaps that part Hallie should take seriously as well. She had a life to get back to in Fort Worth as soon as this was settled, a small class of second graders to teach next year. She had no business involving herself with someone from Greens Hollow. Not now. Ever.

But she would have to deal with Cam—at least until she had Granny's ever-looming problem settled.

Hallie only hoped he wasn't still angry Granny had aimed her shotgun at him—or that he was harboring any plans to press charges against her for it. What penalty did assaulting an officer of the law with a loaded weapon carry? she wondered. She hated to think.

She'd better stay on Cam's good side. And if Granny knew what was good for her, she'd do the same. Cam was holding all the cards at the moment.

Hallie made the small grocery store her first stop, putting off that little talk she knew she had to have with Cam until later. She picked up Granny's mail at the post office, had a bite of lunch at the small deli next door—and had effectively run out of errands.

It was time to beard the lion in his den.

She found the sheriff's office full of boys ranging in age from four to ten, Cam in the midst of them.

"Arresting children as well as little old ladies now?" she asked him as he broke away from the group and sauntered over to where she was standing, just inside the door.

Hallie had never considered herself a sucker for a man in a uniform before, but Cam looked enticing. His shoulders seemed even broader than they already were, his hips leaner, his legs, his stride, more pow-erful.

It would be hard to remember that she didn't need a man from Greens Hollow in her life.

Very hard.

She swallowed a lump in her throat—and thought of her folly with Tommy Lamont. She didn't need to be a little fool again, *didn't need to get hurt again.*

Cam gave her a slow once-over that heated her blood all the way to her toes and back up again.

"Not arresting anyone today," he said, a hint of a smile teasing at his lips. "Just teaching the kids a little fly casting."

And the boys seemed to be enjoying it, too. Reveling in the attention they were getting from this man. Did he have that effect on everyone?

"I wouldn't think that would be part of a sheriff's job description," she said.

Cam laughed.

One of the boys held what looked to be a serious fly rod—Cam's?—and was experimenting with it, no doubt the way Cam had shown him.

What would Granny think if she could see Cam with these kids? This touch of humanness in him? Would she change her opinion of the man?

Hallie didn't want to think what it did to *her* shaky admiration level.

She could easily picture him with a child or two of his own. He'd wear the mantle of fatherhood well. Ever kind, ever patient, loving—that would be Cam.

"Come in and meet the kids," he said, waving her into the room, his gesture, and his meaning, ex-pansive.

Hallie moved forward from the doorway a little shyly. She was used to children. So what was wrong with her?

Was it because these kids suddenly seemed like *Cam's?* That she'd been thinking of him in terms of fatherhood?

She felt like an interloper as they peered up at her. She tried a smile, and the boys responded ever as shyly.

"Hey, guys, I'd like you to meet Miss Hallie. Hallie, this is Grady, Aaron, Eddie, Levi and Garth." He named each in turn, ruffling their hair or giving them a friendly sock on their shoulder.

The boys seemed to love it.

"Say hello to the pretty lady," he added, and in unison, they all did.

"Are you the sheriff's girlfriend?" the one named Garth wanted to know, and Hallie was certain she saw Cam redden slightly.

"Uh, no—Miss Hallie's not my girlfriend. She's just here on...business," he explained.

"What kinda business?" This from Eddie.

Hallie shot Cam a look that begged him not to draw Granny's...alleged activities into the conversation.

He didn't.

"Just, uh, business," he said. "Now, you guys run along—we'll have another session next week, I promise."

The boys trooped out, Garth carefully handing Cam back his fly rod before scooting out after the others. Hallie watched them go, realizing she'd just lost five little chaperones. She was alone with Cam.

And she didn't yet know what she would say to him about Granny.

"I think it's wonderful that you take time with those kids. And it's obvious they've been struck with a bit of hero worship," she added.

Cam brushed her comment away. "Just fostering a bit of community spirit, that's all," he said, uncomfortable with her praise.

The sheriff could add *modest* to his list of other attributes, Hallie decided. "Well, community spirit or not, I for one think it's great."

He carefully, almost reverently, placed his fly rod in the corner beside a worn wicker fishing basket and an old red cooler, as if all were just awaiting a free afternoon of escape. Then he turned back to Hallie. "Before you crown me man of the year, how about you tell me what progress you've made with Pearl."

So, it was back to business. Or at least an easy change of the subject. Hallie took a seat in the chair in front of Cam's desk, the same spot she'd occupied the night Granny had been put in his pokey. Suddenly she knew she couldn't tell him about the recipe. She couldn't bear to see Granny behind those bars again.

If that was wrong, well she just didn't care.

Granny Pearl was family—and family stuck together.

She squared determined shoulders and faced Cam. "I didn't find a still—*if* Granny ever had one," she challenged.

To Hallie, at least, this whole case was circumstantial. Cam had found a few bottles of white lightning, and a still only *he* claimed to have seen.

Hallie's find in the flour increased the odds of Granny's guilt, but Hallie didn't want to think about that at the moment. To her knowledge it wasn't against the law to possess an old family recipe, even if that recipe was one for moonshine.

Cam eyed Hallie closely. He'd been in law enforcement long enough to recognize when someone was lying—or, at least, shading the truth a bit. And he didn't like to be lied to, didn't like to be led down the primrose path. Elise had done that. So had his former partner.

Cam didn't forget easily.

Or forgive.

Hallie had everything to gain by withholding evidence about Pearl. Pearl was her grandmother. Family meant a lot in these parts, he'd learned. In fact, it meant everything.

He dragged a hand through his hair and tried to decide how best to deal with this.

Damn, but the woman had him snowed on Pearl's front porch the other night. *Go home, Cam, I'll search for Granny's still. I'll get the truth out of her.*

He'd let a little bit of moonlight, and one set of foolish hormones, allow him to believe *that.*

Hallie knew *something* she wasn't telling him.

Life had made him mistrusting to a fault, and now was not the time to change his ways. "I think you know exactly where that still is," he said coldly. "In fact, you probably helped the old gal move it. It won't do you any good, you know, to protect her. It'll only get Pearl in deeper than she already is, not to mention yourself in trouble for your...good intentions."

He eyed her with wariness. And suspicion. And Hallie didn't like it. Part of what he'd said was true, she'd get herself in trouble for protecting Granny, maybe even for withholding the fact that she'd unearthed—or un*floured*—the recipe.

But the part about being a co-conspirator, moving some foolish still she'd never laid eyes on, well, that stung. Worse than stung. It got her dander up.

She stood up, needing to put herself on a more equal footing with him—although she was still a good ten inches shy of meeting him eye to eye. "You have your nerve, Sheriff, accusing me of complicity in this." She clamped her hands to her hips. "Just what proof do you have that I'm involved in anything? Or is a person guilty in this county until proven innocent?"

Her eyes snapped with green fire. She really could look meaner than a junkyard dog when she was riled. And Cam had the feeling her bite could be worse than her bark. "Okay, so maybe I didn't quite mean...that."

"You meant *some*thing, Sheriff. You were saying it loud and clear, in fact. Tell me, are you always this suspicious of people?"

"Hey, in my line of work it's a plus." Cam didn't have to defend his attitude. He'd be one poor lawman if he thought everybody he met was a saint. In fact, that kind of thinking could have easily gotten him killed back in Chicago.

It had certainly derailed his marriage, not to mention his trust in his partner, his belief in his fellow cop.

Hallie saw a flash of pain cross Cam's face, his

eyes glitter with some unspoken emotion she'd describe as hurt, then he quickly hid it. Or tucked it aside to brood about later.

She'd touched a nerve. Just who was Cam Osborne? she wondered. And what made him so mistrusting?

In spite of her fury at the moment, her curiosity was piqued. Cam was a man who had old hurts. She'd read it briefly in his eyes. What were they? And why did she have this irrational desire to touch him, soothe them away?

Make him believe there was good in people.

At least *some* people. Maybe Hallie wasn't so innocent right now, but she considered herself a good person. And definitely—make that usually—law-abiding.

As for Granny's law-abidingness, well, Hallie intended to find out the truth about her relative, but until she did, she refused to accept Cam's charges.

"Look, Cam, I told you I'd get to the bottom of this, find out just what my grandmother may or may not be up to, and I mean it. I always keep a promise."

Cam sighed heavily. He couldn't afford to alienate Hallie right now. He'd have to believe her for the moment. He needed her—preferably on his side. He kind of liked Granny Pearl, even if she did consider him lower than a slug in the mud at the moment.

But he didn't want Hallie to have that opinion of him.

He wished he was the kind of man who could look the other way on occasion—but he was by-the-book. Maybe that was colored by his partner's betrayal back in Chicago. Or maybe he'd never been a man who could bend the rules. He didn't know.

All he knew was that he didn't want to see Granny get in any deeper than she already was.

Or Hallie.

"Thanks," he told her. "Thanks for keeping a careful eye out. Things will go easier for the old gal if she stays out of further mischief."

Hallie decided Cam meant it. She had the feeling he had one small soft spot in his cold heart for Granny—though why he should, given *her* attitude toward *him*, she didn't understand.

She figured also that this was as close to an apology as she was going to get from the man for the moment—maybe ever. But what he said was true, things would go easier for Granny if she didn't get into any further trouble.

That was what Hallie wanted as well.

That and maybe a little softening from the man she'd been butting heads with for the past few days.

It was nearly time for the town's July Days Jamboree and Greens Hollow always went all out for the annual event. There were bluegrass bands, barbecue cookoffs, fiddle competitions, possum races, dancing, and the best food the ladies in the county could prepare. It meant extra work for Cam with the crowds that descended on the little mountain town, enforcing security, and corralling the rowdies the partying always seemed to produce.

So why was he taking such a keen interest this year? Why was he counting the hours, anticipating the big celebration? Why was he supervising the putting up of the booths, making certain there would be ample room for dancing, and that everyone would be able to enjoy the bands?

He usually grumbled and groused at the additional workload, added two temporary deputies to the payroll, and made certain all the locks worked on the jail in case it received an influx of inhabitants from the day. Beyond that, he took little interest.

But this year Hallie would be there, and for some reason he didn't want to think about too closely, that made all the difference in the world.

He should recognize that as a danger signal and look upon the town's festivities as just another event. He should confine his contact with the two Cates women to the pending legal situation Granny was in, and nothing more.

But he found he couldn't help thinking about snaring Hallie from the crowd for a dance or two, holding her in his arms, and drinking in that delightful feminine scent of her.

Another kiss might not be out of the question, either.

He hadn't seen or heard from her in almost a week. Trust wasn't something that came easy to him anymore, but he had to trust that Hallie had things under control around Pearl's place, that she might even be getting a few answers out of the old girl. Or at least, the best he might hope for, that Pearl was keeping her nose clean.

At first he feared Hallie might have gone back to Fort Worth for a while, since she hadn't been seen in town for a few days, but last night he'd driven out that way and found her car still parked in Granny's gravel drive. He'd tried to come up with an excuse, a believable one, to stop in, just to see her, just to say hello, but at the last minute he'd decided against it in favor of good sense.

He'd be seeing her soon enough at the jamboree. It was only two days away. And besides, he'd be plenty busy until then, anyway.

"Hey, Sheriff, I got my gun all oiled and ready," Junior Phelps, one of the deputies he'd hired, said as he strutted into the jail.

Cam groaned inwardly. The man put him in mind of Barney Fife. But what Junior lacked in expertise, he made up for in loyalty.

And Cam appreciated loyalty.

"Uh, Junior—why don't you leave the bullets out this year?" he cautioned. "I don't think you're going to need them." The guy was liable to blow his foot off, or worse, someone else's foot.

"No self-respecting lawman goes around without *bullets* in his gun," Junior lamented.

Cam rubbed his right temple, which had begun to pound with a real headache. "I think we'll all be safe enough without 'em." *Safer,* he decided. "Did, uh, you check to see if we have enough barricades to block off the streets around the square?" Maybe with a little luck he could deter "Barney" here from his macho posturing.

The man's shoulders slumped a little, but he reholstered his gun. "I'll do it right now, Sheriff."

"You're a good man, Junior."

Cam shook his head as the deputy swaggered out. He only hoped he hadn't made a mistake in hiring him. There'd been no incident last year, but he'd had to keep a tight rein on the man's...*enthusiasm* for the job.

He returned to the paperwork on his desk. This might be the last chance he had in the next few days to complete it. He'd have plenty to do before the big shindig.

Maybe he'd even get a fresh haircut, have his thick head of hair shaped in that fancy new shop over in Eureka Springs.

Granny Pearl loved a party. All she'd talked about for the past week was the town's upcoming jamboree. Her excitement about the day even bubbled over to Hallie, making her forget, at least temporarily, the trouble Granny was in.

If the woman was busy planning and baking thirty pies for the occasion she wasn't out getting into mischief, Hallie decided, and pitched in to help with the pastries.

Would Cam be at the big event? she wondered, not for the first time in the past few days. Or would he hide out at the jail? All work and no play.

She'd made no excuses to go into town this week; she'd been too caught up in Granny's high spirits, and too busy baking, to spare the time.

Fort Worth held many local events, and so did Dallas, but they couldn't compare to this one small county pulling together. It was something special, something palpably alive.

And she found herself looking forward to it.

By the time the day dawned, Hallie was more than excited—she was downright nervous. The pies were boxed up and ready to be loaded into Hallie's car.

Granny was dressed in her best gingham frock, but Hallie couldn't decide what to wear herself. Suddenly nothing she'd brought with her seemed right.

She should have made a little side trip to Eureka Springs to buy something special, something that would make her look feminine, desirable.

In the end she settled for a soft broomstick skirt that teased around her ankles, strappy sandals and a pale green blouse, open at the neck. She tied her hair up with a matching green ribbon, then thought better of it and let her hair tumble loosely to her shoulders. A touch of pale peach lipstick and she was pleased with her appearance.

"Quit dawdling in front of that mirror, child, and let's get a move on," Granny called, tapping her tiny, but determined, toe by the front door, impatient to be on her way.

Hallie put on a smile. Nothing, absolutely nothing, was going to keep her from enjoying this day, she decided—and only hoped she could keep that resolve.

"Junior Phelps, you move that barricade and let us by. We got a carload of pies here and we ain't gonna haul 'em all the way from kingdom come," Granny barked at one of the town's new deputies who refused to let Hallie drive up closer to the booth-lined street to deliver Granny and her pastries.

The tall lanky man tried to look tough, but failed. "Can't do that, ma'am. The sheriff's put me in charge of these here barricades and told me nobody was to pass."

That put a whole new face on things for Granny.

"The sheriff, huh! Well, you listen here, Junior. That man don't know nothing about movin' pies. I'll deal with him later. Now you let us through or I'll whup your hide good."

Junior seemed to debate which was worse, Granny's wrath or an infraction of his boss's orders. He settled for moving the barricade.

"I'm gonna be in big trouble for this if the sheriff finds out," Junior lamented, but he waved Hallie on through.

Hallie felt badly about this breach of Cam's directives, but Granny was right. Moving thirty pies from the parking area would be a task.

They should have gotten here earlier, and they would have, if Hallie hadn't spent so much time deciding what to wear to the affair.

"I promise to clear this with the sheriff, Deputy Phelps," Hallie said and glanced over at her grandmother looking prim and pleased with herself. "*Granny* will take full responsibility for any of the sheriff's unhappiness," she added, then smiled up at the man, a smile that made him all but trip over his own two feet.

"Hmmph! I don't need you fightin' my battles, Hallie," Granny said as they drove on.

"Well, it seems to me that you do—or you'd still be cooling your heels in that jail of Cam's," Hallie returned sharply, bringing another loud "hmph" from Granny.

All the booths set up around the town's square were brightly decorated. Granny quickly pointed out hers, and Hallie parked the car beside it. They received plenty of help unloading the thirty pies, then

Hallie left, promising to be back once she moved the car.

No sense pushing her luck with Cam—and getting one poor deputy in hot water in the bargain.

She waved to Junior as she slipped out through his staunchly guarded barricades and found the distant parking lot, which was already beginning to fill rapidly. The jamboree looked like it was stacking up to be a real success.

Quaint old trolleys from some of the surrounding tourist towns had been brought in to shuttle the participants to and fro, and Hallie was able to catch a ride on the second one that came along.

Her surreptitious gaze scanned the crowds as she neared the center of activity. She tried to tell herself she was just surveying the scene, but she knew what she was really doing was searching for Cam.

Then she saw him.

He was directing some young kids toward the game area that had been set up on the grassy open lot just beyond the square. Several of the group were teenage girls, and Hallie didn't miss the admiring backward glances they directed at the man as they ambled away.

She couldn't blame them. Cam looked too good to be real in his freshly creased tan uniform. The silver badge pinned to his broad chest glistened in the bright sunlight. His gun and holster settled on his hip like he'd been born wearing it. A light breeze ruffled his hair—Hallie could swear it was a new haircut—and she caught herself wanting to brush it back into place with her fingertips just to feel its silky texture, its brown richness.

Before she could busy her gaze elsewhere he glanced up and caught her ogling him. He smiled, that all-knowing, irresistible smile she was beginning to enjoy a little too much. She should remember the only business she had with Cam Osborne was, well…business. *Granny's* business.

She also should remember that she hadn't told the man all she knew.

She glanced away, but at the corner the trolley stopped to discharge its passengers, and Hallie had no choice but to disembark along with the others.

Cam wasn't going to lose sight of Hallie in this crowd if he could help it. She looked so fresh and tempting in that lime-green blouse, her red hair tumbling over its open collar. Her skirt was long, and flirted sensuously with her slender legs.

He tripped through the crowd that left the trolley, heading off in search of fun and good food, maybe a little music from the bands beginning to warm up in the center of the square. He'd like to have a little fun himself, and only prayed the crowds stayed manageable and orderly, and his deputies proved worth their salt, so he could steal a bit of time with the lady he most wanted to be with today.

Not that he had any right thinking of her in that regard.

He'd vowed to stay on the sensible side of romance for the foreseeable future, possibly forever, but Hallie made that a hard resolve to keep.

Still, if he had any trouble keeping to the straight and narrow he only had to remind himself Hallie would soon be returning to Texas once she had everything settled with Pearl.

Several people called out to him, but he didn't even glance in their direction for fear that if he did, Hallie might disappear from view.

"Hi," he said, coming up to her. "I wasn't sure you'd be here." He put out a hand to assist her from the trolley. She took it a little hesitantly.

A jolt of awareness shot through him at her light touch. He was about to drop her hand when a jostle from the crowd sent her careening into him. He caught her by the elbows and drew her against him for safety.

She smelled like cool rain and new spring grass with a hint of some flowering blossom he couldn't name. He wasn't big on flowers, but he'd be damned if she didn't smell like the most fragrant, the rarest, one he'd like to pluck and keep with him.

"I...I'm fine," she said, drawing away as if embarrassed she'd lost her footing, or that she had to lean on him for support. "And, of course. I wouldn't have missed this day. Does the town really do this every year?"

He smiled. "Someone got it up a few years back—and it took on a life of its own after that. I suppose it fosters a sense of community, gets the folks around here all working together—*and* brings money into the town coffers at the same time."

It also meant a lot of work for Cam, which at the moment he was cursing. He'd much prefer to run off somewhere with Hallie—at least for a while.

Not the best idea he'd had in recent days, but one of the most persistent.

"Save me a dance later?" he asked, hating the fact that he was hanging on her answer.

"Well, I—"

Hallie was about to answer that of course she'd love to dance with Cam later, but before she could get out the words, she saw Granny headed in their direction, spit and fire brimming in her keen eyes.

Cam spotted her, too. "Here comes trouble," he murmured, just for Hallie's benefit. "Maybe I can lock her up at least until I get that dance."

Hallie stiffened. "That isn't the least bit funny, Cam Osborne. I don't want to see Granny anywhere near that jail of yours again. She's old and...and..."

Cam certainly hoped she wasn't about to say "feeble" because he'd have to disagree. The feisty little rebel looked for all the world like she could tear him limb from limb at the moment—and do it happily.

"Sheriff, you done told me you'd keep your distance from my granddaughter. You look like you have every intention of eating her up like she's some tasty dessert. Now what have you got to say for yourself?"

Cam wasn't going to get that dance, he just knew it. Not if Pearl had anything to say about it.

The woman intended to make his life hell.

And he feared Hallie could do the same—in an entirely different way.

Chapter Six

The sounds of the band lured Hallie away from the booth where she'd been helping Granny. She hadn't seen Cam all afternoon, not since he'd deftly side-stepped her grandmother's pointed barb about treating Hallie like a tasty dessert—and reminding him of his promise to keep his hands off her.

As if she were some hothouse plant that would wilt from touch!

Perhaps Hallie *wanted* Cam's hands on her. They were such capable hands, too—big and broad and sure. They could make a woman's skin sing from the slightest brush. What would a night of lovemaking with him be like?

A slow shiver crept along her spine at the imagining before she quietly shoved the thought aside. Granny was undoubtedly right. Any association with Cam—beyond the present, necessary professional one—would only create trouble, trouble Hallie didn't need in her life.

She stepped to the edge of the wooden pavilion in the square where the dancing was in full swing. Just to watch, just to enjoy the band sounds, and the encroaching evening.

"Is your grandmother around?"

Hallie heard Cam's low, male voice; its sexy rumble whispered over her nerve endings. She smiled as he approached warily.

"You're safe," she said. "I left her gossiping with her friends and complaining that the band was too loud. You're not afraid of her, are you, Sheriff?"

He leaned close, so close she caught his clean, spicy scent, could see the soft moonlight reflected in his eyes. "Not as long as I have her effectively...disarmed."

Granny's shotgun. Cam wouldn't forget something like that, one mean weapon aimed in his direction—whether or not Granny would have fired at him. Hallie glanced up. "I'm sure Granny's sorry about that. It's not at all like her."

"Yeah, well, all the same, I'm keeping that bazooka of hers under lock and key." His frown turned to query. "Have you been having a good time?"

"Immensely," she answered enthusiastically. "But I haven't seen much of you."

He leaned back against a tree, one knee bent, his foot resting against the trunk. "I've been busy—crowd control and keeping an eye on those two new deputies of mine. But all's quiet now. I thought I might enjoy the day—or what's left of it."

The best part was left, Hallie thought. The evening

with the stars lighting the night sky, the band in full rhythm, the…dancing.

Cam seemed to read her mind. "I even have time for a dance or two. If you'll oblige me, Hallie Cates?" he asked, his eyes sultry and sincere in his tanned face.

Hallie couldn't resist, even if she'd wanted to. She seemed to be falling under this man's spell, at least for tonight. "I'd like that, Cam Osborne."

This was not a good idea, Cam decided the moment he had Hallie in his arms. She felt glorious there, too glorious. Her soft scent teased at his nostrils, still sweet, still flowery. Her hair brushed his cheek, silky and scented like the rest of her.

The bluegrass band playing earlier had given way to a county band, playing sentimental ballads about love gone awry. Cam knew all about love gone awry—and it wasn't something he wanted to experience again any time soon.

So why did Hallie feel so right in his arms? Was it because she was only a temporary diversion? She would be leaving one day soon? She didn't belong to him—and never would?

So he was safe?

Wrong—he felt anything but safe. Hallie was the kind of woman who seeped into your pores, settled into your heart in a forever kind of way.

She glanced up at him, and he realized he'd slowed the tempo. Slowed, hell—he'd nearly frozen on the dance floor, unable to move. "You want to sit this out awhile?" she asked quietly.

Cam searched around the edges of the pavilion and saw too many eligible vultures just waiting their chance for a dance with her. Relinquishing Hallie to one of them wasn't his idea of an enjoyable evening.

Oh, no. He wanted this woman all to himself.

He gave any hopeful contender a warning glower that threatened bodily pain if any one of them even dreamed of cutting in on him.

"No—I want to dance," he returned. He wanted a hell of a lot more than that from Hallie, but those ideas he might as well shelve forever.

Perhaps that grandmother of hers had been right to warn him away from Hallie. He would do well to take the woman's advice, and he'd consider it—just as soon as he could think straight again.

Cam monopolized Hallie's evening, not that she was complaining, taking every dance with the exception of one, and that he'd given up to a man who was nearing eighty-three, then quickly reclaimed her for one final one.

It felt so good to be in his arms, to feel the scratchiness of his uniform against her cheek, the solidness of his chest, the strength of his thighs, as he pulled her against him. The music was twangy and slow, something sappy and sentimental, but Hallie wouldn't have cared if it was a shuffle as long as she was with Cam, as long as his arms were around her.

They fit together well, as easily as they had the night he'd kissed her on Granny's front porch. She'd noticed it then, and noticed it now. He bent his head and she rested her forehead against his cheek. It was scratchy, too, with the beginnings of a beard, but she liked the way it prickled.

He'd placed her hand at the back of his neck, and

her fingers tangled intimately in his hair that curled over his shirt collar. She closed her eyes and swayed to the music, hoping the song would go on forever.

If Granny could see them now, she'd have a shotgun poised and aimed at Cam's backside for sure. The poor man would be picking buckshot out for weeks—and Granny would be locked up for the rest of her born days.

Hallie only prayed the woman was well occupied with her friends.

Finally the dance ended, but Cam kept one arm loosely wrapped around her as if staking some sort of permanent claim to her as he walked her from the dance floor.

"How about a triple dip of homemade ice cream and a chance to rest those feet of yours I've been stepping all over?" he asked.

He hadn't been stepping on her feet—and if he had, she probably wouldn't have noticed. But the proposal of ice cream sounded great. "I'd love some."

Besides, eating ice cream had to be a little more innocent than dancing, if Granny caught them together. Though she wasn't sure doing anything with Cam could count as innocent. Not with the way he stirred her insides.

"What's your favorite flavor?" Cam asked as they neared the ice cream stand.

"Chocolate," she said, "the richer, the better."

Cam grinned slowly. He knew one more thing about her. She liked chocolate ice cream, and somehow that fact seemed like an intimate divulgence.

"Chocolate it is, then," he said and placed the order for two cones of the same.

He wanted to know more about her, wanted to know her favorite *every*thing. "What else do you like?" he asked.

"Huh?"

"What's your favorite color?" He sounded like a schoolboy out on a first date, but damn it, Hallie had him interested. Much *too* interested—but that he'd worry about later. "Your favorite movie?"

Her hopes? Her dreams? What she wore to bed? The...scent of that flowery perfume she had on?

Or was the scent natural Hallie?

She gave him a small crooked smile. "Blue—I love the color blue. And my favorite movie is...anything old and romantic. What *is* this all about?"

He shrugged slightly. "Just curious about you, that's all."

That made two of them. Hallie was equally curious about Cam. And flattered that he wanted to know more about her, beyond whether or not she'd found Granny's still.

He paid for the triple-decker cones and handed one to Hallie, then found a quiet place to enjoy them, a grassy spot at the edge of the square with a minimum of people milling about. Behind her she could hear the music. Overhead, the moonlight sifted through the boughs of the trees, softening the night, making it seem more romantic than it was. This was just a town jamboree, with a few thousand people from around the countryside in attendance.

But somehow Hallie felt alone with this man.

She watched him sample his ice cream, not allowing a drip of it to trickle down the side. In control—Cam Osborne was in control in everything, even his mastery over an ice-cream cone. That made her shiver slightly. He'd win this tussle with Granny. And if he put his mind to wanting Hallie, she'd no doubt go into his arms willingly.

"Tell me about the kids I saw you with the other day. They seemed...enthralled with you, Sheriff. Do you have that effect on everyone around the county?"

"Just kids, dogs and little old ladies. Uh, make that *some* little old ladies," he amended quickly.

"Not the other females around here?"

He glanced up at her wickedly. "How am I doing with you?"

A little too well, Hallie thought. "You haven't won me over entirely yet, Sheriff."

That was beginning to nudge a little too close to a lie, but Hallie wasn't about to admit it—even to herself. She enjoyed her ice cream for a long, quiet moment.

"The kids," she said again, "you have a real way with them. As a teacher I recognized that—*and* have to admire it." She also recognized good fatherhood material when she saw it. "What about children of your own?" she asked.

"I don't have any."

Hallie smiled. "That wasn't what I meant. Do you want kids of your own one day?"

That might be personal, but somehow she very much wanted to know.

His answer came too quickly, too harshly. "No."

She had treaded where she shouldn't have. One glance at Cam's darkened face, the hard set of his shoulders told her that, but she'd made her way into this briar patch of too-intimate territory, and she'd have to find her way back out.

Gracefully, if she could.

"Not even one—to teach fly casting to?" she pressed.

His ice cream was gone except for the bottom half of the cone, and that he downed in one bite, then gazed over at her. The moonlight glinted on his rugged features, his nose that he might have broken in a fight or maybe on the rough Chicago streets, his chin, strong and square and raised in determination.

His voice when he spoke was flinty. "I was married once," he said. "But it was a mistake, one I *don't* plan to repeat. I was glad there weren't any children to…complicate our lives."

Well, Hallie, that's what you get when you pry— the unvarnished truth. Cam saw children, at least his own, as a complication.

So had Tommy Lamont.

Was it something in the water in Greens Hollow?

No, this baggage Cam had brought with him was from Chicago. What difficulties had life dealt him back there? Whatever they were, they were still there, ingrained in the man.

Cam was good with children. Hallie had seen that the other afternoon. But those boys were *other* men's children, not his own, she remembered quietly.

She'd scraped old hurts in Cam by prying into his life, she realized too late. And she'd resurrected some of her own, as well.

But her own she knew how to deal with—at least on one level. She'd lost a child she'd wanted, even though she'd been young—possibly too young—to know how to raise one.

It hurt now each time she saw a new classroom of children, all bright-faced and scrubbed and eager to meet the teacher, but they soon, each and every one of them, became *her* kids, the ones she wanted so desperately, the ones she hoped to have one day.

She'd do well to remember her life back in Fort Worth. It was where she belonged. Forget any attraction she might have to one good-looking sheriff.

Forget this town that had brought her heartache.

As soon as this mess with Granny was straightened out, she would do just that—go home. And convince Granny Pearl to go with her.

"I—I'm sorry, Cam. I shouldn't have stirred up the past by asking so many questions."

She'd seen the pain that had shadowed his eyes. She wanted to reach out to him—because that was the way she was. She'd never been able to walk away from anyone in need.

But did Cam really need her?

Need anyone?

Cam didn't want Hallie's sympathy. Damn the woman. He didn't talk about himself—or what had happened back in Chicago. Maybe he just ran—ran as far away from hurt and betrayal as he could get.

And he'd thought Greens Hollow the end of the earth.

That was until one pretty, red-haired beauty had come roaring into town to save her grandmother.

Well, she could just take those soft green eyes and

that trembling chin of hers and...and...what? She'd looked so stunned when he'd told her he hadn't needed any kids to complicate his life—or his divorce from Elise.

But then, Hallie was a teacher. She no doubt had one big soft spot in her heart for all rug rats, great and small. Cam did, too, in his own way. He loved teaching the boys around here about fly casting, about sports, about all the other things that interested them, but a kid needed a stable home, stable parents—and he wasn't sure the world was created that way.

At least his world hadn't been.

Her nosiness, and his divulgences about his past, had put a definite damper on the evening—an evening he'd like to get back.

Strange, he'd feared it would have been Granny who'd have thrown the rainwater on the night.

But then, the evening hadn't ended yet.

"Look, Hallie, I guess I'm just not a big believer in home and hearth for...certain reasons of my own. And I'm not sure very many kids in this world get a taste of that kind of life—though, God knows, they all deserve it. Sometimes life is hard and sometimes it's rotten."

Hallie knew about life being hard, downright rotten even. Cam didn't have the corner on that. But it hadn't made her afraid to believe. It only made her fearful, fearful she could make a second mistake, one even greater than the first.

Was that what frightened Cam, too?

"If...if you'd like to talk about it sometime, Cam...I'm a good listener."

He cupped her cheek and let his thumb stray across her lower lip. She felt the roughness of it rasp against her sensitive nerve endings and it sent lightning bolts of charged electricity skyrocketing through her.

How could this man make all her senses come so alive?

"Thanks, Hallie," he said softly. "Maybe...maybe some day I'll do just that."

Then he leaned close and kissed her and those lightning bolts turned into a Fourth of July celebration. The heat of his lips claimed her attention, her sanity too, and she felt herself succumbing.

His tongue traced the softness of her lower lip, slowly, maddeningly, then demanded entrance. She parted her mouth and her tongue brushed his, dueling in a slow dance. She wasn't sure she could breathe or that she wanted to take the time to do so. She wanted only to feel, savor, enjoy.

How could just kissing a woman tear him up inside? Cam mused. But this wasn't just any woman, it was Hallie—and he'd fantasized about this moment since the last time he'd kissed her.

He didn't care that there were people nearby. It was getting late in the evening and couples were pairing off. It was time to stake your claim to the woman you wanted—and maybe in his own way Cam was doing that with Hallie. At least he knew he wanted her.

He also knew he shouldn't.

But those lips, that mouth, were so soft, so inviting. He drew her against him, just for a moment, wanting even more from her. He wanted to haul her off where they could be alone, totally alone, and sample the other soft parts of her. He wanted to make love to her.

Then he heard the voice from hell.

"Cam Osborne, I warned you about touching my Hallie."

The evening had come to an end—in the way he'd feared.

He and Hallie sprang to their feet, and out of each other's arms, both apologetic, trying to put a good face on something that was nothing but obvious—and the old lady wasn't buying it, not for a hot minute.

The best thing Cam could say about the moment was that the old gal's shotgun was locked up tight as a drum. And it was a good thing, too, because she looked none too happy.

"I'd suggest you quit searchin' for this girl's tonsils, Sheriff, and…and go *arrest* someone."

Cam had just someone in mind, but in Pearl's present state of ire he didn't want to tangle with trouble. Besides, she hadn't done anything but warn him about something he should have had the good sense to see for himself.

"Look, Pearl, don't blame Hallie for this. It was my fault entirely. She just looked too damned pretty in the moonlight and…and I, uh, forgot about keeping hands off." There—he hoped he'd cleared Hallie, and that the old harpy wouldn't give her a hard time all the way home.

Hallie glanced up at him. "I can handle Granny myself," she said, "but thanks, Cam." Then she turned to her grandmother. "Come on, Granny Pearl, let's get you home and into bed. You've had a big day.''

Cam watched them go.

Then kicked himself all the way back to the jail.

Hallie took out the small slip of paper with the recipe on it, written in Granny's own hand, and considered it thoroughly. She had to get her mind off Cam and back onto setting things right between her grandmother and the law.

This one tiny piece of incriminating paper spelled trouble for the old girl, Hallie knew. And if it fell into the sheriff's hands Hallie would be in hot water, as well.

They needed a lawyer.

And today was the day to approach Granny with that fact.

In the past three days since the jamboree the woman had calmed down considerably. Almost, *almost,* forgetting the…dalliance she'd caught Hallie and Cam indulging in.

Not that Hallie had put it too far from her own thoughts. But she was determined to stick to business—and that business at the moment was getting legal help for Granny.

She'd phoned Cam this morning—strictly a professional call—and had gotten the names of two excellent attorneys in the area. One was over in Eureka Springs, the other a little farther afield.

Now all she had to do was convince her grandmother it would be the wise thing to do to see one of them.

Cam had wished her good luck in getting Pearl to

go. His tone had a hint of a chuckle buried in it, but she knew he meant it when he said he hoped all would go well. There was always just the slightest catch in his voice when he spoke from the heart.

But she didn't need to be thinking about Cam, that catch in his voice, *or* the way the man had kissed her.

"Granny Pearl," she called out to her as the woman entered the cabin after feeding her goats their morning snack. "We need to talk."

Granny set her pan down with a clatter. "If this is any more of your nonsense about my de-fense, girl, you can just forget it," she snapped.

Hallie ignored the remark and proceeded on. "I have the names of two good attorneys in the area. You can have your pick of them, but there'll be no argument about going. *To-day,*" she added.

"Now, just you listen here, Hallie Cates, I don't need no highfalutin lawyer. I ain't afraid of the judge. I done powdered that man's bottom before he was growed," she snorted.

And she wasn't above reminding the poor man of it in his own courtroom, Hallie was sure.

"Granny Pearl, somehow, some way, we're going to get this whole mess cleared up, and when we do you're going back to Fort Worth with me where I can keep a closer eye on you."

"When pigs fly, girl."

Perhaps Hallie hadn't broached the subject correctly. She tried again, using a bit more finesse to her tone.

When that didn't work she tried cajoling the old

woman. That brought only a glower and a suggestion that Hallie could just pack up her bags and go.

Hallie was sorely tempted, but she was in this to the bitter end.

She decided the better part of valor would be to abandon the topic for the present. Along with the idea of a lawyer to represent Granny.

The old gal was stubborn.

And when she got her dander up Hallie might as well retreat.

She did.

She took a walk, just to think. And to smell the dogwood.

It didn't take long before she began to feel the peace of the place, the redbud trees blooming in profusion around her, the birds chirping their merry songs, the squirrels scampering in the brush alongside her, the warm sun overhead.

The countryside was lovely, she had to admit, as she paced tranquilly along the dusty road that ran past Granny's property. And she knew Granny would miss all this terribly if Hallie took her back to Fort Worth to live.

She could understand the woman's reluctance to leave here, leave her roots, her home, her two cute little goats, but Hallie worried about her, too, living here all alone.

She should be with family in her declining years—and Hallie was the only family she had.

This place boasted no nearby medical facility, no doctor closer than a winding, thirty-mile drive away over dangerous roads.

Her grandmother needed someone to see she ate

properly, got her rest and ample exercise. And that she stayed out of mischief.

Her thoughts had carried her farther than she realized, and suddenly she glanced around, not certain where she was. The afternoon had warmed up considerably, and she was beginning to feel a little light-headed.

Heavens, she'd worried about Granny, when perhaps she should have been paying a little attention to herself.

How many turns had she made? The roads in this area ran in no sensible direction, but meandered, pleasantly sometimes, here and there.

When had she seen the last house? The last weathered road sign? Not even a car or truck had rattled past—which was not unusual around here.

Hallie glanced about, looking for something, anything, even remotely familiar. She longed for a tall, very cold drink of water—and a road map.

In lieu of either, she settled for a patch of shade, courtesy of an old, leafy oak tree beside the road. She'd rest there for a while, then try to retrace her path.

But she knew the wrong turn could carry her farther out of her way. Granny would begin to worry, and she didn't want her to be upset.

A short while later Hallie was certain her guardian angel was looking out after her. Off in the distance, heading in her direction, was one very dusty sheriff's car.

And unless she'd wandered into the next county, that sheriff had to be Cam.

Chapter Seven

It had been quiet around the sheriff's office today—
too quiet—so Cam had lit out of there. All he'd had
to think about had been Hallie and the way her lithe
body had felt against him the other night, the way
she'd kissed him back, allowing his not-so-gentle in-
vasion of her sweet mouth. Giving as good as she
got, as he remembered.

The woman had one helluva lot of passion bottled
up inside her, just waiting for some guy to release
it—and damned if he didn't want to be that guy. But
that, he knew, would get him into trouble.

Of the variety he didn't need.

Besides, he'd promised himself no entanglements—and that was a promise he intended to keep.

Despite Hallie.

Despite his ornery hormones.

To save his sanity he'd piled his fishing gear into
the sheriff's car and stole away for an afternoon of

fishing. He'd felt only moderately guilty about abandoning the office. There hadn't exactly been a crime spree going on around the little town, so he'd figured he'd hardly be missed.

And besides, if he'd sat around the place all day, twiddling his idle thumbs, his thoughts, and his *wants,* would turn to Hallie.

Now he was headed back. He would lock up the jail and set off for home for a nice quiet little fish fry and a cold bottle of beer or two. He'd kick back and—

What the hell!

Cam stomped on the brake and took a closer look at the woman standing in the middle of the road, waving her arms at him to stop. Unless he missed his guess the woman was Hallie—looking a bit fatigued, a bit dusty, but tantalizing, nonetheless.

Trouble, with a capital *T,* some sentient part of his brain allowed. But his hormones bucked, his breath caught, and a soft smile melted onto his lips.

Wherever, whenever, he couldn't deny he liked seeing her.

He drew to a stop beside her, rolled down the car window, and tried to look stern. "What the hell are you doing out here, miles from Pearl's place?"

Hallie let the air-conditioning from inside the patrol car cool her hot face and prayed Cam had something cold to drink with him. Anything.

She didn't even notice his cranky reminder that she'd wandered farther afield than she'd intended. The shot of cool air just felt too good, and she was too overheated to allow her temper to flare.

"Can I hitch a ride with you back to Granny's?"

she asked. "I'm hot, tired, thirsty—and not at all in a good mood right now."

There, that should warn him to just back off with the lecture.

He looked so darned put together, while she must look a wretch. Relaxed, calm, cool, and unthirsty. He also looked handsome—but at the moment she wasn't sure she had the energy to properly appreciate that.

Later. Later she would remember how much like her knight in shining armor he seemed, riding to her rescue on his white steed—well, patrol car, anyway.

Same thing. Almost.

She didn't wait for his answer but swung around to the other side and slipped into the seat beside him. Between them was a powerful-looking rifle in a stand, on the dash a police radio with a myriad of buttons, but all Hallie saw were the air vents, which she quickly aimed in her direction.

"What brought you out here—if I might ask without riling your mood further?" he quizzed her.

"I took a walk."

He only gave her a look, an amused, *knowing* look.

"Okay—I took one turn too many and got lost."

She waited for his laugh, but it didn't come. Instead he reached behind the seat and flipped up the lid on his battered old cooler, rummaged inside for a moment, then handed her an icy, *wet* can of orange soda.

Hallie fell on it with one swift grab, then, before she popped the top, gave a cautionary glance back at the cooler. "You don't keep the smelly fish you catch in there, do you?"

If he said yes, Hallie wasn't sure she'd refuse the soda. She was just too thirsty.

And hot.

Fortunately, he shook his head. "The 'smelly' fish are in the trunk. In fact, I was thinking about grilling them tonight, maybe enjoy a cold beer with them." He smiled over at her, and the lines at the edges of his eyes crinkled in his sun-darkened face. How long had he spent on a creek bank? "I, uh, wondered if you'd care to join me? I'm pretty good with a barbecue grill."

Maybe it was the thought of the cold beer, but Hallie was tempted to say yes. She could think of a million reasons she should refuse the invitation—the least of which was Granny's objection to her keeping company with this man; the most significant, her wayward attraction to him.

Then she remembered that Granny was busy tonight—her quilting group again. Hallie would be on her own for dinner. And why cook when she could get a free meal?

Cam waited for her answer. She took a long swallow of the orange drink, enjoying the iciness of the cold can, and the way the pop quenched her dusty throat.

She lowered her drink and considered the offer. "Do I have to clean the fish?"

Cam laughed, a hearty...*sexy* laugh. "Only if you want to. I'd never ask a woman to do that—especially a *city* woman."

Did he have to remind her she was a city woman?

But she loved his gallantry about men doing the fish cleaning.

"Then I accept."

He smiled—as if he were glad she had—then put the car in gear and set off toward Granny's at a leisurely pace. After a few miles, he made a turn, and things began to look familiar again.

"I'm not sure how I managed to get so lost, but I do remember coming by here. There's the old school up that drive," she said. "I passed it earlier and noticed it had been boarded up."

Hallie was certain it wasn't just for the summer. It had a look of *permanent* abandonment, as if it hadn't been used in some time. Granny hadn't mentioned its closing in any of her letters—and she'd intended to ask her about it when she got back from her walk.

Walk. If Cam hadn't come along when he had, she'd probably have gone around in circles for some time on these twisted roads. She knew her landmarks, of course, but somehow she'd lost sight of them, her musings about Granny—and Cam—leading her heaven only knew where.

"The old place closed the year before last," Cam said. "The students now attend another school some distance away. Those who didn't drop out, that is," he added.

"Drop out?"

Cam grimaced. "Yeah—some of the kids can't spare the extra travel time because they're needed at home—or so their parents feel. It's a fact of life for the families around here, everyone is expected to pitch in with the chores, help make the ends meet."

"But, Cam, that's terrible. Isn't there some way?"

"To keep them in school?" He sighed deeply. "I talk to the kids—and to the parents—try to tell them how important it is to get a solid education, but sometimes it's just not possible. For some around here, it takes every family member to keep body and soul together." He turned to gaze at her. "I'm sure you have a dropout rate in Fort Worth. From drugs, poverty—the things that tear up a kid's life."

Cam cared. Hallie heard it in his voice. He'd no doubt seen much back in Chicago that tore at him. They weren't immune to drugs or poverty back in Fort Worth either, but a cop saw so much more of life—the raw, the dangerous, the ugly side of it. Was that what had jaded Cam?

Or was it something more personal?

Something closer to his soul?

She wished she could ask him about it.

"I'm sorry to hear the school closed down," she said instead. "It was always the lifeblood of this little town."

"It was," Cam agreed.

Just then Pearl's place came into view. Cam turned into the long drive and hoped the old tyrant wasn't looking out through those curtained windows to see him arrive with her granddaughter in tow.

Hard telling what she'd be thinking he was up to with her now.

"Uh, maybe I shouldn't go much farther," he said. "I don't want to provoke the old girl."

Hallie grinned. "Yeah, well, I thought I'd play it safe, too, and avoid mentioning where I was having

dinner tonight.'' She reached for the door handle.
''Oh, Cam, can I bring something tonight?''

Only herself, Cam thought. ''Not a thing,'' he said
and wondered what kind of trouble he'd stirred up
for himself by inviting Hallie to his place.

She was everything he'd once wanted in a woman.

And everything he shouldn't have.

Hallie had ignored Cam's answer that she not
bring anything to the fish fry. She'd never been a
guest who showed up empty-handed for a party.

She arrived at his place with a few fresh-made
biscuits of Granny's and a jar of her special jam that
she smuggled out of the old girl's pantry, feeling
only slightly guilty that she was carrying it to the
enemy camp.

She'd found Cam's house easily enough, follow-
ing the directions he'd given her—but when she saw
him she wasn't so sure she should have come.

He'd scrapped his uniform in favor of a comfort-
able-looking pair of shorts and a white polo shirt that
showed off his tan to perfection.

His legs were strong and sinewy, with a fine smattering of silky dark hair covering them that glistened
in the setting sunlight. His sensual brown eyes
searched hers through thick dark lashes, and a tempting smile teased at the corners of his sexy mouth.

Perhaps it wasn't too late to take a rain check on
dinner, she thought with a hard swallow.

She moistened her lips and wondered if he'd buy
that—then realized she'd seem rude. Besides, he
probably wouldn't allow her to retreat.

And she didn't really want to retreat.

"I, uh, brought some biscuits," she said, holding them out as if they were a peace offering.

He smiled. "I told you it wasn't necessary—but I'd be crazy to turn down some of Granny's baking." He paused before taking them. "She didn't, uh, spike these with a little arsenic, did she?"

Hallie smiled. "If she knew I was absconding to your place with them, she might have."

The woman would not be pleased to know Hallie was spending the evening with Cam, she knew. But then, Hallie was an adult—and she didn't need permission to go where she wanted.

Besides, Granny was taking this feud with Cam a little too far. Cam liked the old gal, despite his teasing to the contrary. He wasn't Granny's enemy.

He wasn't Hallie's enemy, either.

"I guess I'm still not her favorite person, huh?"

Hallie grinned. "Don't take it personally."

He placed the biscuits and jam on a round patio table, picked up a pair of silver tongs and set to work turning the fish on the grill.

"That woman holds a grudge worse than anyone I've ever arrested," he said. "Did you get her to agree to see one of those lawyers?"

"Not...yet."

He glanced up. "Do I hear a bit of desperation in your voice?"

Hallie sighed. "Let's just say holding a grudge isn't Granny's only personality flaw."

"You came up against a brick wall, huh?"

"A brick wall of stubbornness. She didn't use to be this...this...cantankerous. It must go with age."

He gave her a sympathetic smile. "Older people

see it as fear of losing some of their precious independence, their own right of decision making. They sometimes don't take kindly to the younger generation making suggestions about how they live their life.''

Hallie sighed. ''I guess I did come on a little too forceful, giving her an ultimatum.'' She paused. ''Not only about seeing an attorney, but...''

''But...?''

The temperature had dropped a few degrees with evening, and the air was pleasant, a soft breeze blowing. She sauntered over to stand beside Cam, absently watching the fish turn to a golden brown under his expert barbecuing skills.

''I insisted once this legal mess was settled that she move back to Fort Worth to live with me. I got a real earful, I can tell you.''

Cam glanced away at her comment. He didn't want Hallie to read what was in his eyes. He'd known she'd go back home, and all too soon. He just didn't like hearing her say so.

At least not yet.

What was happening to him here? This was the first time he'd invited a woman to his house. It was his retreat—his place to heal from his wounds, his scars.

But if he allowed himself to feel what he was beginning to feel for Hallie, he'd soon have new wounds to deal with.

And he hoped he was smarter than that.

''Would you mind grabbing the pepper grinder for me? These fillets should have a touch more,'' he said, needing to root himself to the reality of grilling fish, and off the thought of Hallie leaving. "It's just inside. In the kitchen. Counter to your left," he added.

"I'll find it," she said.

Hallie was glad to be of use. She gave Cam a smile and headed for the back door of the small split-log house he lived in. It was the perfect size for a bachelor, and well built. Less rustic than Granny Pearl's old place.

And a whole lot more modern, she decided, when she stepped into the big kitchen. Oak cabinets lined the walls, and tall bar stools sat before a long eating counter that divided the kitchen from a large living room.

She glimpsed a fireplace, a big comfy-looking sofa in front of it—and wondered what it would be like to curl up there with Cam on a cold winter evening.

Unable to stop herself she wandered into the living area, touching this chair and that, a lamp with a deep green shade, a book Cam had been reading—a crime novel, which didn't bring about any surprise—a well-worn toss pillow, a small tin of Brazil nuts he probably enjoyed munching on, several well-read sporting magazines.

There were no old family photographs on the mantel or anywhere else in the room, not even one of a friendly, favorite old dog. Perhaps he had a few pictures sitting around in the bedroom—but she had no intentions of straying in there.

All the same she wondered about family, Cam's. Did he have brothers, sisters? He'd mentioned he'd been married once, but from the chilly tone she remembered in his voice, she didn't expect to see some special old photo of any former wife sitting around.

She was snooping—there was no other word for it.

And she should get herself back to the kitchen and find that pepper grinder he'd asked for. Cam's personal life was no concern of hers.

Still, she wished she knew more about the man.

Because she was beginning to care about him?

That sent a tingle through her, a swift reminder that she needed to be on guard against her own feelings.

She found the grinder right where Cam had said it would be, and started for the back door, then noticed the plates and silverware stacked beside it. She picked them up, too, and carried them out.

She would set the small patio table for dinner—it would give her something to do while Cam was busy grilling.

Cam glanced up to see Hallie coming out the back door.

Lord, but the woman could look enticing. Her hair was particularly curly tonight, as if she'd used a curling iron on it for just that special…feminine look. If that was her intent, it had worked. Hallie was nothing if not feminine.

She had on a touch of makeup, not that she needed any, but it gave her a slightly sultry allure Cam decided he liked. Slim white jeans sheathed her legs, and a pale yellow sweater accentuated her small breasts.

"I brought the plates," she said softly. "I'll do the table."

"Thanks." The single word came out slightly strangled.

Hallie affected him.

"Here's the pepper," she said, handing him the small wooden grinder.

Her scent was something sweet—and too close for comfort. Their hands brushed briefly as he took the pepper from her, and she blushed.

He affected her, too.

He drew in a breath and sprinkled the fillets generously.

"Tell me about the school closing," she said as she set the plates around, anchoring the napkins down with the silverware. "Was it a financial decision, a lack of money...?"

"No, not entirely financial," he said, "though there's certainly a huge expense in keeping a small school like that open." He loaded the grilled fish onto a plate, then dug in the coals for the foil potatoes he had baking.

He was glad to focus on conversation, rather than on Hallie, and how tempting she looked.

"There was also the problem of no teacher."

"No teacher?"

A lightning bug danced around her in the twilight that was fast descending. No doubt the creature found her as tempting as he did. "It's not an easy task teaching grades one through eight. That, plus the fact that nobody wanted to stick around this small burg."

Cam brought the fish and the potatoes to the table Hallie had finished setting, then disappeared inside for the coleslaw and the promised beer. While he was gone Hallie thought about what he had said.

She recognized how difficult it would be to find a

teacher willing to teach all eight grades—but even more difficult, finding one who'd agree to the primitive school conditions of Greens Hollow—no matter how much the town *needed* a school.

There were so many advantages available in a metropolitan area, that simply couldn't be found in an out-of-the-way, rural setting—computer labs, language classes, special school plays, creative classes, field trips to the science museums, planetariums.

The learning possibilities were endless.

It was just the advantages she wanted for her own children—when she had them. What parent wouldn't?

And what excitement would there be for a single young teacher around the area—*if* one agreed to stay. Beyond the…hunky sheriff the town could boast of, she amended.

That gave Hallie pause. Yes, some young teacher would definitely find the man enticing.

Enough to consider hanging around?

It would be the only job perk the position might offer.

Hallie didn't want to think about some pretty slip of a girl snatching up Cam Osborne. But it wouldn't happen, anyway—the school was closed, and no doubt would remain so *permanently*.

Just then Cam came out of the house, salad in one hand, two bottles of beer in the other, and Hallie had no time to think about it further.

"Ready to eat?" he asked.

Hallie nodded, having to admit to herself that she was famished, and that Cam's cooking endeavors smelled wonderful.

He lit a candle on the patio table, then doused the porch light.

"To hold the bugs at bay," he explained, apparently wanting to assure her the move wasn't for romantic purposes.

Which was fine with Hallie.

It wouldn't do to go getting any romantic notions about this man—not when she didn't intend to hang around long.

And not when Cam wasn't in the market for a wife or children of his own.

It was better to keep him off-limits and confine any husband-seeking ideas she had to Fort Worth, or maybe Dallas. She'd been burned by this town once before—and she wasn't about to let it happen again.

"Another beer?" Cam asked when dinner was finished and the dishes washed up and put away.

He reached for the refrigerator handle, but Hallie shook her head. "None for me, thanks."

What she'd had already had gone to her head.

Cam had turned on the stereo earlier and it played softly in the living room, something slow and romantic. A candle burned there, too, and Hallie didn't think it was for bug control.

Instead it lent an ambience to the room, a softening of the masculine in Cam's furnishings.

"I like your place," she said. "It suits you."

He glanced around as if to see it through Hallie's eyes.

"Think so? I seem to spend a lot more time in the office than I do around here—but I suppose it's home."

Another slow song began to play in the distance.

"Do you miss Chicago—I mean the excitement of a bigger place?"

She wasn't sure what she was asking—or why—it was just that she was trying to reconcile the man from the city coming to a town like this.

"I meant it about this being home, Hallie. I'm happy here—if that's what you're asking. This place has a certain...peace to it. It's why I don't think you'll have any luck getting Pearl to leave here. I'm sorry to tell you that—I know it's not what you want to hear."

"It's not, Cam."

Not at all. How could she keep an eye on Granny from such a distance away?

And Granny had no one else to look after her.

But Cam didn't know Hallie's determination when she wanted something. Granny would adjust—in time. And Hallie would bring her back for visits now and again. Maybe for the jamboree each July. She'd bring her husband, her children.

But somehow that scenario didn't play right in her head, and Hallie wasn't exactly sure why.

"Cam, I—I should go."

He reached for her hand that had gone for her purse, stilling it, then laced his fingers through hers. "One dance first," he said.

Her hesitation cost her. He pulled her against him and tugged her arms up around his neck, then drew her to the center of the room.

Hallie was sure she'd never danced with a man in a kitchen before and dancing with Cam—any-where—was sensual. The music was soft, coming from the living room, and distant enough to sound ethereal to her ears.

There was no angry Granny to rescue her this time, no crowds milling about to keep things chaste between them. It was just the two of them, frighteningly alone.

Fort Worth seemed a million miles away at the moment, her resolve to return there even farther. Cam was the most exciting man she'd ever danced with, she was certain, the most exciting man she'd ever kissed.

And she'd be a little fool to succumb to him, she reminded herself sharply. Cam didn't want the same things she did—home, hearth, advantages only a metropolitan area could offer.

And children.

Hallie wanted babies. Lots of them. She wanted to teach them everything, show them the world, give them all the love she had in her to give.

Cam was content with Greens Hollow and the little it had in the way of opportunities. He wanted to run the town in his own by-the-book way, drowse beside a creek bank for relaxation—and dance with a woman in his kitchen.

Though she had no complaints about the latter at the moment. She had to admit, it was nice. More than nice—it was...wonderful.

He tipped his head dangerous inches lower and brushed a kiss across her ready mouth. Heat flamed to life within her. Her blood raced. And her heart thudded so loudly she was certain he could hear it.

"You're beautiful, Hallie," he whispered against her lips, apparently unaware of her wildly beating heart, but knowing only too well how to bring out every crazy sensation her body was capable of—and bring it to raw awareness.

He was hard with desire as he drew her closer, cupping her buttocks with his big hands. Her breath caught and her senses fled. The music faded to a distant throb—or was that her own need, her awareness of nothing but Cam?

Finally he released her and the room spun back into some kind of off-kilter focus. The music had ended, the song over. Before a new one started she drew in a steadying breath. It was shaky.

Cam smiled. "Yeah, me too," he said. "I'm not sure what you do to me, Hallie, but I think I had better walk you to your car—or I'll end up taking you to bed and keeping you there until sometime next week."

She smiled, secretly liking the thought, despite realizing just how dangerous that was. "Granny would have the militia out after us," she said.

He brushed the flat of his thumb across her cheek, releasing a slow, wistful sigh. Granny wouldn't stop him, she knew—not if making love to her was strong enough on his mind. He was giving Hallie an out— and she knew she'd better take it.

She reached for her purse and slipped the strap over her shoulder. "I—I had a lovely time tonight, Cam," she said softly.

"Me, too."

He drew her toward the door. "Now, you get your little fanny on down that road or I'll rescind my chivalry."

* * *

Cam watched the little Subaru speed off down the drive and tried to focus on the Texas plates adorning the back end. They should be one damned good reminder that Hallie would be leaving here—and soon—but he wasn't sure he could remember that for long. Certainly not when he tried to fall asleep tonight and ended up staring at the ceiling and thumping his pillow until the wee small hours of the morning.

He let out an oath and started for the back door. Maybe he'd go in to work—get his mind off the woman who was capable of setting him on fire.

Chapter Eight

Over the next few weeks Granny stayed busy with her quilting ladies. Hallie was a little curious about the woman's keen interest in the pastime—and the group, in general. Maybe even a little hurt that Granny seemed more intent on the activity than she did in spending time with Hallie.

It occured to her that her grandmother might be up to some sort of mischief, but she quickly decided her suspicions were unfounded.

What possible trouble could six little old ladies get themselves into?

There was safety in numbers. And Hallie should feel relieved that Granny had something...circumspect to fill her time.

With Granny thus occupied, Hallie was at loose ends and ended up seeing more of Cam Osborne than was probably wise—definitely more than Granny would have approved of.

She made several trips into town to run errands—errands that her grandmother had been neglecting of late—and stopped in Cam's office to chat. Sometimes they had lunch together at the small deli next to the post office—though Hallie worried that these casual "dates" might get back to Granny.

Twice Cam took her night fishing, a diversion Hallie found she enjoyed, perhaps because she caught the biggest fish, perhaps because the man she was with let her boast that she had bested him. Hallie knew only too well that her catch was beginner's luck, but she appreciated Cam not pointing that out.

Tonight Cam was taking her to dinner at a new restaurant over in Eureka Springs—a special night out. Though, with Cam, any night seemed special.

She hurried to dress, knowing he'd be arriving at any moment—and she wanted to look her best. Granny had already left for the evening—her quilting group again.

Again Hallie had a few doubts about what her grandmother might be up to—but quickly quelled them.

Granny had promised her no more mischief—and Hallie had to believe her.

Cam hadn't questioned her about Granny lately. He seemed to accept that she knew nothing about her grandmother's alleged activities—or the still that, according to him, had conveniently disappeared.

Hallie had even let it slip her mind that she hadn't totally come clean with the man, that she hadn't "'fessed up" to finding Granny's old moonshine recipe in the flour.

Cam was beginning to trust her—and she didn't

want to stir up trouble when it wasn't necessary. Besides, the recipe was probably of no consequence.

Later. Later if it became important she would tell him.

She slipped into a white sundress with a smocked bodice and billowy skirt. She twisted her hair up off her neck and secured it with a clip. Showing off the nape of her neck looked…sexy, she decided.

She liked the effect, perfect for a romantic evening in Eureka Springs.

Romantic? Hallie sighed. It wouldn't be a good idea to get romantic notions about a man she'd soon be saying goodbye to. She took the clip out of her hair and let the curls fall to her shoulders.

Cam had strived to keep their time together light, carefree, almost—but not quite—hands-off. So had Hallie. And tonight would not be a good time to change the status quo.

It would be hard to think about leaving here, of never seeing Cam again, but that thought Hallie shoved to the back of her mind. She liked her life back in Fort Worth—the school where she taught, the children, *especially* the children, her comfortable little apartment, her friends, the many things there were to do there.

Once school began she'd quickly be back in the swing of things, too busy to think about Cam—and the way the man could kiss. She'd forget how they'd danced together, how she'd bested him with a rod and reel on a quiet creek bank with the cicadas chirping and the water roaring over the rocks, the smell of the dew-laden grass. She'd forget the brush of his mouth against hers and the way her heart tripped all over itself.

Life would be back to normal again, except that Granny would be with her.

Tonight was just a night to share with Cam, a night to have a little fun, a little sophistication in her life that was sorely missing in quiet Greens Hollow.

Just then she heard Cam's car tires crunch on the gravel drive. She slipped into a pair of sandals with beads across the toe and a slight heel, took one final glance in the mirror at herself and headed for the door.

Cam was standing on the porch at the edge of the cabin, idly staring out over Granny's back property. Was he still trying to decide whether or not the old girl had a still hidden away out there?

"Cam..." she said softly.

He spun around, but when he saw Hallie, the furrow across his forehead softened, and a wide, *pleased* smile broke across his lips. "You look...terrific," he said appreciatively.

So did he.

He had on a pair of pale tan chino slacks, freshly creased, and a crisp navy shirt, open at the neck. His hair was brushed to a fullness, the ends still a little damp around the ends as if he were just straight from the shower.

And that smile smeared across his face was definitely sexy—and all for her at the moment.

He escorted her to his Cherokee and helped her up into the front seat, his touch just this side of electrifying.

She'd have to be on her guard tonight against her wayward senses.

Look, don't touch.

Cam had been reminding himself of that ever since he'd picked up Hallie this evening. He wasn't at all sure what was happening to his resolve to keep his objectivity around this woman. Certainly the past two weeks had placed him near the breaking point.

And sitting across the table from her now, watching the moonlight play across her face, had him sucking in a breath and trying to hang on to sanity.

The restaurant was one of his favorites—not that he had much time to try it out often—on top of a refurbished old building on one of Eureka Springs's winding downtown streets.

In the 1880s, when Eureka was in its heyday, it had been a hotel built on top of one of the mineral springs the town had been famous for. Now it housed unique shops for the tourists, and this pricey establishment perched on top.

The food was better than he'd had back in Chicago, the trendy burg capable of stealing away a terrific chef or two from the big cities. With the summer tourist season in full swing the restaurant was crowded, the streets below teeming with people of all ages who'd come to enjoy the little town built on a mountainside.

But Cam's observations were limited strictly to Hallie—and the way her smile lit up every closed-off portion of his heart, portions that should remain closed. If he were wise.

He'd kissed that mouth more than a few times

lately—and it still had him intrigued. So did the way the candlelight turned her skin above that sexy white sundress to a warm peach. And those tiny straps that curved over her bare shoulders, straps he'd have one helluva time keeping his hands from untying later.

Dinner over, they relaxed, enjoying the remainder of their wine.

"I like this town," Hallie said. "When I was a little girl I loved to come here and hike the hilly streets, drink from the cool springs. My dad always brought me."

Hallie had never talked about any other family members, except for Pearl. Somehow Cam had assumed the woman was all she had. "Tell me about your parents," he prompted.

He thought it a safe enough topic—and maybe it would keep his mind off those tiny straps.

"My...dad was killed when I was eight, in a light plane crash. He had his own—and loved to fly it."

"I'm sorry, Hallie. I didn't know."

She shook her head. "It was a long time ago— but the memories of him are very much with me. My mom and I went it alone after that. Then a few years ago she married again."

"Does she live in Fort Worth?"

"Not anymore. They—she and her new husband—have a motor home and they travel. I hardly ever see them." She smiled. "What about you?" she asked.

"My parents live outside Chicago—I don't see them often, either. I can rarely get away from the sheriff's office for a vacation."

"Any brothers or sisters?"

"A brother," he admitted. "Back in Chicago. He's a cop, too. We were in neighboring precincts. Kenny's the best Chicago's ever seen."

Her green eyes were soft, probing, capable of tearing up a man's soul.

"Why'd you leave, Cam?"

He'd expected talking about family would bring up other questions...the personal ones he tried not to think about. How could he tell her what he'd never told anyone? He hadn't even told Kenny. But Kenny had heard what had gone down, knew why Cam couldn't talk about it yet. Maybe ever.

He took a hard swallow, hoping it might loosen his tongue, but the words still stuck in his throat. He leaned back in his chair, and let out a low sigh.

"I had a partner who was on the take, Hallie. I don't know if you understand what that can do to a cop—especially when the man had been a partner. But it...did something to me, taught me a hard lesson. A bitter one."

Her eyes looked solemn—as if she *could* understand. Or wanted to. "Tell me about it, Cam."

Of course she'd press. It was the way Hallie was—and he'd opened this whole can of worms up in the first place by asking her a few personal questions.

He took another swallow of wine. Maybe he needed to tell *someone*—and Hallie was the only person he'd consider sharing the painful part of his life with at the moment.

He'd told what he knew to Chicago's internal affairs, then had quietly tendered his resignation. What had gone down between Lazaro and himself had hurt—hurt even worse than his breakup a few months later with Elise. But it had only cemented in his mind that it wasn't good for a man to trust anyone.

"There was a drug deal my partner and I had been working on, but what I didn't know until that night was that Lazaro was looking out for his own interests. He…he nearly got me killed.

"I knew after that I wouldn't be a good cop. I wouldn't be able to trust another partner—and a cop has to be able to trust the guy working alongside him—and vice versa."

Hallie glanced down at her drink. So that was what had made Cam so mistrusting, why he'd tolerate no lies, no subterfuge, why he was so by-the-book.

The fact that she hadn't told Cam all she knew hadn't escaped her. But was now the time to confess? She wanted to—but suddenly she was frightened. Cam would not be very forgiving.

"And your wife? Ex-wife—was she part of the reason you left Chicago, too?"

Maybe this was safer territory. Hallie hoped.

"Lazaro's betrayal hurt far worse than anything Elise could have done, but yeah. I'd thought Elise and I had a good solid marriage. It turned out we didn't. It's not entirely her fault. It's not easy being married to a cop. I got caught up in my work—and I shut her out of it. These few years here in Greens Hollow have given me a little perspective about that."

"And now…do—do you still have feelings for Elise?"

Hallie had to know. She didn't think he did—but what did she really know about how Cam felt on the inside? Tonight was the first time he'd talked to her about himself to any extent.

"What Elise and I had together is long dead," he said quietly, resolutely, and Hallie was sure she heard herself let out a slow sigh of relief.

She knew how love could die. How one betrayal could change everything. Tommy's betrayal and losing the baby hadn't exactly bolstered her quotient of trust either.

But Hallie wasn't afraid to try again. With the right man this time.

She only wished Cam could be that man. But he wasn't—and no amount of foolish wishful thinking could change that.

She understood Cam a little better, knew who he was and what he was about. Why he felt the way he did about trust, about life, the law...

She needed to tell him about that recipe of Granny's she'd found, level with him about what she knew.

But just then the waiter appeared with their bill and Cam paid it.

"Come on, Hallie," he said when he'd dropped a tip onto the table, "let's walk. I want to show you this town."

The moment for Hallie's honesty had passed.

Cam hadn't been sitting in on the local poker game lately—Hallie had been occupying a good deal of his time—but tonight he decided he'd try his luck. Besides, he needed to pull back and think, think about just where he and Hallie were going with this relationship.

Relationship? How the hell could it be that, when she was planning to leave soon?

Still, a relationship was exactly what it was beginning to feel like.

Last night had been damned nice. He hadn't minded talking about himself, once he got going. He'd never known a woman he could talk to so easily—but with Hallie, he could.

He found the guys in the usual place, the storage and catch-all room at the back of the general store. Henry Tull who ran the small emporium hosted the party several times a month, and Cam felt badly when he missed. He liked the men who gathered to play—and the poker sessions were about the only thing that passed for male camaraderie around these parts.

Besides, he usually won.

"Well, well, well—decided to turn loose of Miss Hallie for a night out with the boys, huh?" Henry Tull exclaimed as Cam walked through the door.

Jake Grooms danced up from his chair and slapped him on the back with a broad wink of his good eye—the other eye he'd lost in a hunting accident years before. "Great goin', Sheriff. She's a pretty one—but you'd better be danged fast on your feet if old Pearl gets her gun out after you."

Cam refrained from telling Grooms it had already happened.

"What is this? The whole town knows every move I make these days?" Cam asked, narrowing his eyes menacingly at the motley group he'd once thought were his friends.

He was beginning to have second thoughts.

The men only hooted louder.

"Have a seat over here by me, lover boy, I'll give you a few pointers on how to keep that little female happy," Charlie Yates, at forty-eight the youngster of the group, razzed.

Cam decided maybe coming here wasn't a good idea. He also wondered just how much about his relationship with Hallie the small-town busybodies had picked up on.

"Hallie and I are just friends," he explained, though even to his own ears that pat answer sounded a little weak.

The guys thought it humorous, too, and the hooting and razzing began again in earnest. Cam was beginning to get irritated.

"Hey, guys, I thought we were here to play poker," he snapped.

He thought of Hallie and the way she'd looked last night at dinner, her green eyes wide and solemn, the moonlight—and candlelight—making them look lustrous, making *him* feel like he was the only man in the world at that moment.

And when he'd kissed her good-night... He'd known he had to take a serious look at his feelings, a serious look at where he was going. No woman had ever tied him in knots the way Hallie could—and he didn't know what the hell he was going to do about it.

"Yeah, we're gonna play poker," Grooms said.

"If you can keep your mind on it long enough to play a hand."

The guys guffawed again, and Cam began to consider making a hasty exit until the heat died down—if it ever did.

"Just deal, guys," he barked.

The evening wasn't much better later on when Cam got home. He'd managed to clean the guys out—but only by sheer force of will. His mind *had* been on other things, as Grooms had inferred. Damn the man. Cam knew he had a few questions he needed answers to, such as—just what was it he wanted from Hallie?

She wasn't someone a guy could have a quick fling with and then discard—he'd figured that out early on.

Hallie was special. And it might well be that he was falling in love with her.

Lord, but that made him nervous as hell. He spent the remainder of the night—and the next few nights—thumping his pillow and trying to decide just what he was going to do about this pretty redhead very much ensconced in his life.

Hallie had made no bones about returning home after Pearl's pending legal problem was settled in court—a problem Cam had foolishly brought to light. He only had himself to thank for the situation he found himself in. But Cam didn't want to think about Hallie leaving, didn't want to think about what it would be like not having her around.

She'd been like a breath of fresh air to his life—and to this town. She didn't like it here, he knew—but she was just what the town needed.

Possibly what *he* needed.

But damn, how could a man be sure?

He couldn't afford to make another mistake regarding his life. This time he might never recover.

Hallie stayed close to home the next few days. She'd had a wonderful time with Cam the other night, but he'd stirred some shaky emotions in her, emotions that if Hallie had an ounce of good sense she'd squelch—and quickly.

She hadn't come back to Greens Hollow to tumble head over heels in love—not with anyone.

What had happened to her good sense? What had happened to lessons learned? Lessons learned the hard way?

She had her life on track, a happy track—and she didn't need any handsome man from this neck of the woods derailing it. She had a teaching contract in Fort Worth. In three more years she'd be tenured. She had plans and goals and an incentive to be the best possible teacher she could be.

She wanted children—several of them—which she intended to have as soon as she met the right man for her.

Cam Osborne didn't fit the bill, not by any stretch of the imagination.

She needed to quit thinking about him, needed to put some sense and substance back in her life—and that was what she intended to do.

Granny was out again this evening. Time weighed on Hallie's hands. She'd finished up the supper dishes. There was absolutely nothing on television.

Maybe she'd read. Hallie had tucked two paperbacks in her suitcase, one a romantic fantasy, the other a juicy murder mystery. Since she hardly needed more fantasies to fill her head, she'd read about murder—a little grit and mayhem on this warm summer night.

She dug in her suitcase for the book, but instead her hand ran across a plump envelope of letters she'd brought with her.

She sat down in the middle of her small bedroom and dumped them out on the hardwood floor in front of her. Maybe these little masterpieces would bring reality back into sharp focus for her—the goodbye letters from her class each child had written her before they'd gone off for their small summer adventures, letters she'd brought with her to read when she had a quiet moment.

Well, tonight was quiet—and she needed her life tilted back toward reality.

She picked up the first one reverently and read:

Dear Miss Hallie
I luv you. Thanks for teeching me all bout bugs and stars and math and stuff.
I'm going to the beach in Cala—Californya this summer. I'm going to swim in the big oshun.

Luv, Justin

Hallie's eyes misted as she tucked the letter back into its hand-made paper-and-glue envelope and picked up the next.

Dear Miss Hallie
Can you teach me agin next yeer?
Your the best Teacher I ever had.

Love, Emily

She reached for another, then another, reading
each one in turn. Some of the kids had included
drawings of their favorite summer activity, their pet,
their family.

Her heart wrenched and tears welled up. The children defined who she was, where she belonged.
What she needed to go back to.

There was only one problem—she was afraid she
was falling in love with Cam. And she wasn't sure
how she'd be able to say goodbye to him when it
was time to leave here.

Dear Miss Hallie
Yur my prettyest teacher.
See you next yeer.
I hope yur summer is fun.
I luv you.

Dustin

Hallie let out a deep sigh and tucked the letters
away. All of them. She couldn't read any more tonight. Dustin had wished her a fun summer. And
she'd had fun—fun with Cam. But fun wasn't without complications.

Only in childhood was it ever that way.

She packed the letters back in her suitcase, found
her book and pulled it out—but she didn't feel like
reading it.

She glanced at her watch, wondering why Granny

wasn't home yet. It was getting late—and Hallie needed someone to talk to, someone with a shot of wisdom, someone to remind her she'd strayed into danger here once before.

That she was straying into danger again.

When nine-thirty came, and Granny still hadn't appeared, Hallie began to worry in earnest. She checked her watch again and decided she'd better phone a few of Granny's friends.

She found her phone book and placed a call, then another—and another. Not one of her quilting crew answered. A sinking feeling settled into the pit of Hallie's stomach.

And it weighed against the doubts about Granny she'd been having the past few weeks.

If she hadn't been so caught up with Cam lately she would have been more vigilant. She wouldn't have let Granny's late nights slide, she'd have gotten a few answers out of the old girl.

If Granny Pearl had herself mixed up in some sort of mischief...

Hallie sighed. She'd promised Cam that wouldn't happen.

Just then her gaze fell on Granny's sewing basket beside her old rocker. She dropped the phone and started toward it. The sinking feeling in her stomach was fast hitting bottom.

Just as she thought.

Granny's quilting needles were there—*all* of them. So were her favorite thimble, her spools of quilting thread, the small pair of scissors she always used.

Hallie groaned. The old woman and her friends were up to something—and Hallie would bet it wasn't something good.

Chapter Nine

This time Hallie wasn't going to waste efforts trying to get answers out of her grandmother, the *sphinx*. She was taking the bull by the horns. She was turning private detective.

Hallie had never done this before, but tonight when Granny Pearl left—*sans* quilting needles again—Hallie tailed her. She kept the little Subaru some distance behind Granny's green jalopy, not wanting those keen eyes catching a glimpse of it in the rearview mirror.

The old fox headed toward town, then took a detour that doubled back to the abandoned property smack dab next to Granny's. Sam Wilhelm's old place, Hallie remembered.

Several other equally antiquated clunkers had already gathered. The quilters, *en masse*. And Hallie would just bet they didn't have quilting needles, either.

Each had parked their vehicle out of sight of the road, fairly hidden by a clump of tall pines. The casual observer wouldn't have noticed them—but Hallie wasn't a casual observer.

The tiny group of gray-hairs took off through the piney woods and underbrush with Granny in the lead—and Hallie in hot pursuit, a safe distance behind.

Hallie didn't feel the slightest qualm about following her relative. Granny Pearl had been released into her custody; she was *her* responsibility—which Cam would be all too happy to point out to her.

Besides, she loved Granny—and she didn't want anything to happen to her.

She moved slowly, careful not to snap a twig and alert the ladies to her presence. She'd just bet their ears were as keen as their penchant for getting into mischief.

Hallie cursed under her breath as her toe caught in a rabbit hole and she twisted her right ankle. But it didn't slow her down. She kept up with the crew ahead of her, though each step hurt like hell.

The pain made her more determined than ever to find out what the old biddies were up to.

She'd turned detective for the night, and that was what she intended to do—detect.

Their route wound this way and that until it neared... Granny's property—the back edge of it. Not far from the area Hallie and Cam had searched and found nothing.

Just then the group stopped. Hallie did, too, hiding behind a large oak tree, which afforded her a clear view of just what the little outlaws were doing.

What they were doing was removing five or six dead tree branches to reveal...

Hallie had never seen a still before in her life, but she knew in an instant that's what it was. The still Cam had seen earlier, and Hallie hadn't been able to find.

And now she knew why.

Granny and her cloak-and-dagger friends had spirited it away onto neighboring property, where Hallie hadn't thought to look for it.

She groaned and thought evil thoughts about six little old ladies.

The group was adept at assembling the pieces. Hallie waited and watched with growing ill humor until the apparatus began to gurgle and bubble. They were making moonshine—there was no doubt about it.

Hallie had caught them red-handed—and unless she did something, they were all headed for jail.

She stepped out from her hiding place behind the tree and marched toward the brew crew, advancing on them like a conquering general.

A gasp went up when they saw her approach.

"*Oh, my!*"

"*The jig is up!*"

"*Hallie!*" This last from Granny. "What are you doing here?" she demanded, though Hallie thought that should have been *her* question.

"Hello, ladies," she said as sweetly as if she'd just joined them for afternoon tea. "I thought I'd stop by and see how your, um, *quilting* is coming along." She marched over to the crafty little still and took a deep sniff. "Refreshments, I see."

The ladies shuffled uncomfortably. A few of them had the good grace to look chagrined. But not Granny. Her chin raised brazenly. "You were spying on us, Hallie Cates," she said. "How could you do that?"

"I prefer to call it...detecting—and how could I do it? Because I care. Because you are all in deep hot water the moment word of this gets back to the sheriff. Because..."

Hallie was so angry she couldn't think of another reason. She wanted to throttle each and every one of them.

Instead, she surveyed the still like a demolition engineer, then jerked a large coil piece from the apparatus, thus ending the gurgling and bubbling—and hopefully incapacitating it for good.

Then she turned back to the group and faced each one squarely. "Ladies, you are out of business."

"It's just *rheumatiz'* medicine," Miss Hattie, the town postmistress explained, when Hallie lined up fourteen bottles of their makings on Granny's kitchen table.

The coil from the still, along with a few other vital parts, were safely locked away in Hallie's trunk to ensure that the clever little group didn't resume operations again any time soon.

She had assembled the ladies at Granny's, intending to give them a stiff talking-to—and to make them understand what they were doing was against the law and could send them up the river for ten to twenty.

And most in this group didn't look like they had ten to twenty left to spare.

"That's right," explained Cora, "we was just providin' a service to the county. Most of the people around these parts are old, and our squeezins makes 'em feel better."

Hallie sniffed a bottle of the stuff. She'd just bet it made them feel better. In fact, a few ounces of it and they'd feel no pain whatsoever.

"Well, I'm really sorry I broke up your little, um, pharmacy here, but I can't let you do this," she explained. "I can't let you all get caught and put in jail. You'll just have to find something else to cure your aches and pains, girls. Sorry."

A collective grumble went up from the group—but Hallie was sticking to her guns.

Throughout the stern lecture Granny was strangely quiet, and Hallie hoped the old girl wasn't hatching some new method of operation in her mind.

Finally she spoke up. "I s'pose you're plannin' to tell that sheriff 'bout this the minute our backs are turned, aren't you?" she said with a loud sniff.

The old gal was clearly put out with tonight's developments, but that was just too bad.

As for her remark...

Hallie had no idea what she should do about informing Cam. He'd be mighty unhappy if she didn't, if she kept this to herself. On the other hand, if she told him, he'd probably put the women in jail—and then how would Hallie feel?

Not very pleased with herself.

Cam was a man who went by the book. Hadn't he made that clear to Hallie? He wouldn't easily look the other way, not where the ladies were concerned.

Her brow pleated and she rubbed her temples

where a headache had begun to pound. Why did she always end up in some dilemma where Cam was concerned? At odds with the man?

"I'm going to have to give this some consideration," she said. "I just can't think right now. But I promise you, before I'd inform the sheriff of *anything,* I'd give you fair warning."

It was the most she could offer them.

She'd boxed herself in, but good, by stumbling onto Granny's little undercover operation.

And, at the moment, she was terribly angry with her relative for putting her in that position.

Hallie began to relax as the week progressed. She'd averted disaster.

Granny was home every night, feeding her two goats, baking cookies and other goodies, and generally behaving herself. She'd even agreed to go and talk with a lawyer about her pending court case. They had an appointment in two days.

Hallie was pleased.

Her relief was undeniable.

Hopefully there would be no further trouble—and Cam wouldn't even need to know about the events of the other night. In fact, Hallie had decided to keep it to herself. She'd handled things quite effectively on her own. She'd shut down operations, dismantled the still, and disbanded the ladies.

She'd even gotten rid of the last remaining supply the women had on hand. She couldn't do anything about the bottles the old girls had already sold off—and that worried Hallie some. But she didn't want to think about that tonight.

She was feeling too pleased with herself, certain that all would finally be all right—that her world, and Granny's, would at last be sane again.

"C'mon out on the porch, Granny Pearl. The stars are beautiful tonight. I want to just sit and look up at them."

The night was, indeed, beautiful—even her upsetting feelings about Cam seemed distant at the moment.

"Why, we ain't watched the stars since you was a little girl," Granny said, appearing at the door, a reminiscent smile on her face. "But I think we need some o' my fresh-baked cobbler to go along with all that stargazin'."

Hallie agreed. "Sit down, Granny—I'll dish us up some."

Yes, she was glad she hadn't bothered Cam with the events of the other night. Hallie had handled it all just fine herself. In fact, Cam should be proud of her for her efforts.

Cam had arrested eleven people in town for drunk and disorderly conduct—and the night wasn't over yet.

"Don't tell me, let me guess. This jug of ninety proof is some of Pearl Cates's concoction, isn't it?" he said to the latest group of prisoners he'd ushered into his establishment.

"Tha' li'l old gal's hooch is the best in Ark'n'saw," Jed Brewster answered, a commercial recommendation that didn't exactly put Granny's case in good stead at the moment.

At least not with the sheriff.

"Yup," his brother Jonah added. "Pearl knows howta whip up a batch o' squeezins that'll put hair on any man's chest."

It was too bad it didn't add a little hair to these men's *heads,* Cam thought with a grimace at the elderly group. At least then it would have been useful for something besides stirring up brawls in otherwise civil, law-abiding individuals.

Some of the old boys were already trying to sleep it off, others were singing, and Jed and Jonah continued to praise Pearl's talents and attempt to wheedle Cam into leaving the old gal alone to make her moonshine. After all, what was it hurting?

Cam wished they had *his job* just for tonight.

He rubbed his aching temples and headed out to try to restore law and order to tiny Greens Hollow. If he could get his hands on Pearl Cates at the moment he'd wring the old biddy's neck.

And Hallie... He'd thought he could count on her, thought he could trust her, but she'd blindsided him.

And that was one thing he'd promised himself he wouldn't let happen. Not a second time.

What would she have to say for herself?

He wasn't even sure he wanted to hear her excuse. He'd come here to remote Greens Hollow—the last sensible place on earth, he'd thought—hoping to find some peace in his life, some sanity, but what he'd found instead was more dishonesty.

He'd reached out to Hallie, opened up to her, only to discover she couldn't be trusted any more than his old partner—or his ex-wife.

Damn it all, he only had himself to blame for this. His brain had warned him to keep his distance from Hallie, from any female who might intrigue him, but when it came to Hallie Cates his heart and his insistent set of hormones had led, instead.

By the time the night was over, Cam had put in six more hours rounding up brawlers and general, all-around rowdies, imbued with Granny's firewater.

What did the woman put in the stuff?

And how much of it had she sold?

Cam could be busy for days.

He cornered another rough-and-ready group and herded them into the patrol car and carted them off to jail to sleep it off along with the others he'd apprehended.

The whole lot of them would have riotous headaches in the morning, he predicted. And they'd be full of apologies.

He supposed Hallie would have her apologies to offer about this, as well, apologies about Granny's moonshine disturbing the town's peace and quiet. *Cam's* peace and quiet, too.

But those apologies wouldn't mean a thing.

They'd just be more hollow words.

By morning the news of Cam's arrests was all over town. Hallie had heard it from Miss Hattie, who'd phoned Granny bright and early.

Granny had tried to keep from telling Hallie, but Hallie had demanded to know the details.

The details were not good.

Cam had put in a hard night. Half the county, it seemed, had ended up in his jail—and he was going to blame Hallie for it.

At least for not being honest with him.

A short while later Hallie appeared at the sheriff's office. Though the men had all been released to their families and sent home to suffer their hangovers out of range of Cam's earshot, the place still reeked from stale booze.

Cam felt a secret delight when Hallie wrinkled up her pretty nose at the smell.

The woman had it coming.

And Pearl Cates had *worse* coming. He hoped the judge would throw the book at her.

Still, a part of him harbored a tinge of sympathy for what Hallie was going through with Pearl—and for having to endure the unpleasant smell of this place.

Cam had had enough of the place, as well. He flung open a few more windows and ushered Hallie outside where a soft fresh breeze stirred and the morning sun slanted down. A few wildflowers bobbed in the small patch of earth near the front entrance. Their fragrance was a delightful counterpoint to the smell of a jail that had housed drunken men for the night.

"Thanks," Hallie said as she settled herself demurely on a bench up against the front of the building.

Did she have to look so fresh and pretty? The sun turned the red in her hair to golden fire and her green eyes looked misty and troubled.

He redoubled his efforts to hold on to his anger.

"I know you must think this is all my fault," she said hesitantly and toyed with the faint crease in her white denim shorts.

Her legs were long and tanned beneath them. Her

toenails, poking out of her open sandals, were painted a pearly pink. Her breasts rose and fell a little more rapidly than was normal beneath her Dallas Cowboys T-shirt.

And Cam struggled for calm.

"I suppose you didn't know a thing about this, that Pearl is innocent, and I'm off my rocker for even considering that your sweet, *charming,* little grandmother had anything to do with the firewater the men were drinking last night."

He was working up a full head of steam.

"We had an agreement, Hallie. You were going to find out what Pearl was up to and report back to me. I thought I could trust you to do that."

Her breasts rose again, this time convulsively. Cam averted his gaze and studied a furry squirrel searching for a buried nut in the grass.

"I was, Cam. But I couldn't find the still—at least not at first. Then…then I found Granny's recipe hidden in the flour canister and suspected she might not be as innocent as she claimed—"

"Her recipe?" His eyes flashed to hers. "When was this? How long ago? And when were you going to tell me about it? Or were you?" His gaze scanned her face. "You weren't going to tell me."

Hallie glanced away. She didn't know how she could make him understand her reasons for keeping quiet, how she could make him understand she was afraid for Granny, afraid the woman would end up behind bars again.

Cam was angry. His eyes glittered. The veins stood out in his neck. He pushed a hand through his hair, showing his frustration with her, with Granny, the whole, entire situation.

She just wished he didn't look so all-male in that uniform, so *in authority*. It frightened her. *He* frightened her.

"I'd intended to tell you, Cam, but..." She spread her hands in a gesture of helplessness.

"I trusted you, Hallie." His tone was cold, flat.

She knew how he felt about trust. He'd told her about his partner, what had happened back in Chicago. But this was different.

At least in Hallie's eyes.

"This isn't about trust, Cam. It's about loyalty. My loyalty to Granny Pearl. She's my grandmother, family. *My* family. I couldn't let her go to jail again."

Cam stood in front of her, not giving an inch. "So you ignored the law and appointed yourself judge and jury. That's great, Hallie, just *great*. It seems you didn't feel you could trust me, either."

His hand dragged through his hair again, and he turned his back to her. To contain himself?

"There's more, Cam."

He might as well hear it now. He'd learn about it later, anyway—and then it might be worse for her. For Granny. Maybe she should have told him sooner, but she loved her grandmother.

He turned around, his gaze raking her face. "Let's hear it, Hallie. *All* of it."

"While we were together—I mean, you and I, Granny was busy with her own agenda, and...being secretive about it. I should have guessed something was up, but her preoccupation meant she wasn't questioning what I was doing, who I was seeing."

His eyes softened for a moment, as if he might be remembering a few of those nights they'd had together, a few of the kisses they'd indulged in, what they were beginning to mean to each other. At least, Hallie thought they were beginning to mean something to each other, something…special.

"The other evening I followed her. She met up with a few of her friends, unearthed the still where they'd hidden it—"

"The still. Just as I thought. Where was it? *Where*—?"

Hallie wasn't sure she knew this man. At least this was a side of him she'd never seen before, a side she wasn't sure she totally understood.

"Sam Wilhelm's old place," she returned, just wanting this to be over. She didn't like Cam's interrogation of her. He was a lawman, first, last and always.

"Wilhelm?" He gave her a questioning glance.

"The property next to Granny's," she explained. "Sam died some years ago, and it's been abandoned land ever since."

He nodded that he followed. "Go on."

She drew a shaky breath. "It was there—the still, under a pile of brush. The group assembled the parts and made some of their brew. I stepped in, dismantled the thing and sent the ladies packing. After I gave them a stern lecture."

He paced in front of her. "But you didn't see fit to call me, even to tell me about it after the fact?

I'm the sheriff here, the *law,* not you, Hallie—despite your good intentions.''

"I couldn't tell you, Cam. I love my grandmother.''

"Then, damn it, Hallie, you shouldn't have promised you would. Who are these ladies? I want names.''

Hallie had made another promise—this one to Granny's friends. Whether it was right or wrong. Whether Cam liked it or not. "Not until I talk to them first, Cam. I'll get them to come in and face the music on their own.''

"Yeah—sure you will.'' His tone said he didn't believe her. "I could lock you up for not cooperating, for withholding evidence, you know.''

Hallie stood up. "Then do it, Cam. If that's what you want to do—do it.''

Damn the woman, Cam thought. She stood there so brazen, so tough. Locking her up wouldn't solve one damned thing, he knew. She could be as contrary as Pearl.

He'd get nothing from her if she refused to talk.

"Go home, Hallie, go home before I change my mind and toss you in a cell and throw the key away.''

He turned from her and marched inside, leaving her standing there, staring after him.

He was angry—too angry to deal with her at the moment.

Angry—and hurt by her betrayal.

He slammed over to his desk and slumped into the chair behind it. Suddenly he hated this job. And he wished he'd never set eyes on Hallie Cates.

Chapter Ten

"**M**oonshining?"

The lawyer peered over his glasses at Granny when Hallie finished explaining the reason for their visit to his office. A slight smile had twitched at the edges of his mouth once or twice—and Hallie knew he'd been struggling to hang on to his professionalism.

It might have been humorous to Hallie as well—if she weren't so...personally involved.

"That's the charge," she returned, giving her grandmother a sidelong glance. The woman was perched a little too stiffly on the edge of her chair. Granny wasn't comfortable being here, explaining her case to a lawyer and asking for help. She seldom asked for help from anyone—Hallie included. Only when her back was against the wall.

And Hallie would have to admit that was where the woman was at.

The lawyer took off his glasses, polished them thoughtfully for a moment, then slipped them back on. "I didn't know there was anyone around who knew how to make spirits these days," he said, studying Granny Pearl again. "I thought all the old…talent had died."

"Well, young man, this old talent's very much alive—and I make a darned good sauce, if I do say so myself," she snapped back.

"Granny, I, uh, wouldn't go around boasting about it—given the circumstances you're in," Hallie warned, her gaze narrowed on the tiny woman.

"I didn't mean any offense, Miz' Pearl," the attorney said respectfully. Ward Buchanan was his name. A middle-aged man with a slightly balding dome pushing through the top of his hairline. "My great grandpappy made some fine stuff in his day. I just wasn't aware there were any stills in working order around here, unless maybe they were in a museum."

Granny had been eyeing him warily, not sure she wanted to place her trust in someone she hadn't known from the time he was in knee pants. But Ward Buchanan came well recommended, so Hallie hoped she'd relax and trust the man.

They needed his help. Especially after Granny's makings had disturbed the town's peace in a big way the other night.

"Are you sayin' I'm relic age? My still should be sittin' 'longside some old dinosaur bones?" Granny grumbled, her forehead crimped into a frown.

Ward Buchanan leaned across his polished maple desk, looking eye to eye with his client. "Miz' Pearl, you might need to place that still of yours alongside dinosaur bones—considering the trouble you're in. Now, I suggest we start planning your defense."

Yes, Hallie thought, they needed to get down to business.

Granny was in serious trouble. And she and Hallie were in this alone. There would be no kind word from Cam—and definitely no leniency.

His coldness the other day had cut into her like a knife. She'd hoped he might understand how she felt, why she'd tried to protect her grandmother, why she hadn't told him all she knew—even though she understood how he felt about that.

But Cam had shut her out, sharply, coldly. The anger she saw in his face, the mistrust she'd read in his eyes, had hurt. She'd hoped he might at least try to see her side, understand that Granny was family. She'd hoped family meant something to him, as well. But Cam had shut himself away from feelings, from understanding. It was all black or white to him. There was nothing in between.

She didn't condone what Granny had done—but she wasn't sure Cam knew that. Her grandmother had broken the law and would have to pay the consequences for it.

And Hallie was paying a few consequences herself.

She'd lost Cam, and that hurt more than she'd ever imagined.

She'd made a mistake of the heart in this town once before, and now, it seemed, she'd made another.

She wished she'd never come here. But then, she

hadn't had a choice. She'd needed to come for Granny's sake.

She hadn't needed to fall in love with Cam, however. *That* she could have avoided—if only she'd remembered past mistakes.

Her folly had only hurt her—and it hadn't helped Granny, either.

The consultation with the attorney took another thirty minutes. Ward Buchanan queried Granny about a few more facts of the case, then offered his four-point plan, which would center on Granny's age, the fact that this was her first offense, her good standing in the community and that Granny was contrite.

"What do you think will happen with her?" Hallie asked him when he was through. She liked his plan; short of the *insanity* defense, it was the next most plausible.

Buchanan steepled his fingers in front of him. "She goes before Judge McBain. He's not a man known for going easy on the people who appear in his court, by any means, but I think he'll take our plea into account. She'll no doubt get off with probation and some community service." Then he turned to Granny. "I would advise that you *not* remind Judge McBain that you'd once powdered his now overly large backside, however," he warned. "Unless you want a stiffer sentence."

Granny snorted, started to say something saucy, then apparently thought better of it and clamped her mouth shut.

Hallie hoped that was the way she remained in the courtroom, as well.

* * *

Cam shuffled a few more papers on his desk, not really seeing what was on them, not having any burning desire to work on them. The only desire burning in him at the moment was taking back his attitude last week with Hallie.

He wished he'd handled things differently—but how, he didn't know. What Hallie had done, she had done. And Cam couldn't trust her.

Trust meant a whole lot to him. It meant everything.

And Hallie knew that. Hadn't they talked about it that night at dinner in Eureka? How much had she known then—and hadn't told him?

It all burned in Cam's gut. It made him cranky as hell during the day and kept him awake every night. No, it was missing Hallie that kept him awake.

Until his eyes felt like two raw sockets and his gut like a knotted hot poker.

He'd let his guard down somewhere along the way—and allowed Hallie to sashay right past. He rubbed his forehead, cursing the drumming headache that had been a persistent part of his life the past week, cursing his own damned foolishness, his...misjudgment for coming so close to falling in love with the woman. Close? Oh, no—close wasn't an accurate assessment—he *had* fallen in love with Hallie.

And now his only problem was figuring a way to get over it. To forget everything she'd meant to him, forget that sweet smile, the way she'd felt in his arms...the way she kissed him back so full of passion and giving.

Oh, damn! He gathered up the papers in front of him, unread, and tossed them willy-nilly into his in box to look over later. There wasn't a thing in them that couldn't wait until he'd gotten over this disease of the heart. In a thousand years or so.

Cam heard the office door creak open and glanced up, happy for a diversion. But that happiness was short-lived when he saw five primly dressed old ladies inching their way inside.

Miss Hattie, the postmistress, was in the lead. She strutted closer, the others in a tight trail behind her.

"Ladies..." Cam nodded a greeting, feeling certain that trouble was in the offing. "What can I do for you?"

They consulted each other silently for a short moment, then Hattie spoke up. "We've come to turn ourselves in," she said.

Like he'd thought, *trouble!*

He didn't need this.

His eyes darted from Hattie to the others, each in turn. "All of you?"

"All of us," they chorused as if they'd spent the last two evenings rehearsing it.

Cora James put out her arms. "You may handcuff us if you like, Sheriff."

"Yes," the others agreed.

Cam glanced at five pairs of arms, proud but trembling in front of him and wondered how these frail little ladies had ever managed to transport a still over hilly terrain. And what they were doing here in his office—tonight—when the last thing on his mind was arresting anyone.

Hallie. He'd bet she had something to do with this.

She'd said she'd talk to the women. Was that the reason they were here, waiting for him to slap the cuffs on them?

Cam groaned. All he wanted to do was go home and drown his sorrows in a cold can of beer and try to forget the way Hallie looked in the moonlight, that misty smile of hers, the softness of her skin.

"We intend to stand side by side with Pearl in the courtroom," Hattie said. "We're all as guilty as she is—so you can book us, Sheriff."

Book? The ladies had been watching a little too much television, Cam decided. And as for them being equally guilty... They may have been in on Pearl's little enterprise—but Pearl was the ringleader. There was no doubt about that. It was *her* recipe. *Her* still.

Cam didn't want to be the one to figure out degrees of guilt. At the moment he was very much wishing he'd never arrested Pearl Cates.

"It's late, ladies, why don't you come back tomorrow," Cam suggested evenly. Maybe by then he could figure out what to do with the women.

"Oh, no," they cried.

"We want to be arrested," insisted Miss Hattie.

Cam shoved a hand through his hair. That wouldn't get him named the town's favorite citizen, he knew. But what was a sheriff to do? "Okay, ladies, you're all under arrest." He cleared his throat. "And released on your own recognizance. But— don't leave town."

As if the fivesome would go more than thirty miles away—but it sounded official.

"Aren't you going to fingerprint us?" Cora asked, not certain the group was getting the full treatment.

Why did the law have to be so damned difficult? Cam rubbed his jaw, feeling his five o'clock shadow thickening. It was getting late—and he wanted to go home. "You ladies got any priors?"

They consulted each other, then shook their heads.

"Good. Then we can dispense with the fingerprints." He hoped they didn't ask about mug shots.

They didn't.

"Are—are we free to go then?" Hattie asked, clearly disappointed there wasn't going to be more—probably so she could tell her great-grandchildren.

"That's it, girls." He stood up and ushered them toward the door.

When they'd finally tottered out into the night Cam let out a weary sigh. At least the evening had taken his mind off Hallie.

Temporarily.

But later his thoughts would be back, he knew—along with the torment those thoughts inflicted.

Maybe when this was over, he'd think about taking a vacation. A long one. To someplace exotic.

Someplace that might make him forget.

For the past week Hallie had avoided going into Greens Hollow because she didn't want to run into Cam. Forgetting the man was hard enough without seeing him looking so tempting, so handsome, in his uniform. But today Granny insisted on running errands.

When Hallie suggested they drive to Harrison for those errands Granny gaped at her. "That's miles out of the way. What's got into you, girl? You been hangin' around this cabin, stickin' to the place closer'n glue.'' She narrowed her eyes at her grand-daughter. "It's that sheriff, isn't it? You're tryin' to avoid him—and it's all because of me.''

Granny had been moping ever since they'd returned from the attorney's office the other day, convinced she'd made a fine mess of their lives because of her moonshining. Hallie had wanted Granny to put on the brakes some, to behave and forget her wayward ways—but strangely she found she missed the feistiness in the old woman. Granny wasn't being Granny when she was glum and blaming herself, and Hallie didn't want to add to that by letting her think her problem with Cam was totally because of her.

"No, Granny, Cam and I got too…close. That part was my fault,'' she said. "You'd warned me not to get mixed up with someone from here again. Cam and I are…too different, but I failed to see that. It really had nothing to do with you.''

Only peripherally, Hallie thought. Granny's activities may have been the trigger, but the problem went deeper. It went to who Hallie was and who Cam was.

She wanted a man who'd understand why family was important, who'd be there no matter what—who wouldn't run away when someone was in trouble. Like Tommy Lamont had done. She wanted a man who wanted to be part of a family, who wanted children and love—and who didn't hide his feelings behind pain and unforgiveness.

Cam would never be that man, no matter how much she wanted him to be.

"Just how serious did this get between you and Cam Osborne?" Granny wanted to know.

Serious enough to get her heart broken, Hallie thought. Serious enough she wasn't certain she'd get over the man any time soon.

"Look, Granny, don't worry about me. I'm tough, remember? And I got it all from you."

Granny gave her a glance that said she wasn't sure Hallie looked so tough right about now.

They went to Greens Hollow to do Granny's errands. All the while Hallie kept an eye out for Cam. When she didn't see him, she wasn't sure whether she was relieved or...disappointed.

She left Granny discussing the price of a chuck roast with the proprietor of the general store and went outside to wait and to read the magazine she'd just bought. She'd only flipped through half of it when she saw Cam coming out of the sheriff's office.

He saw her a quick moment later, hesitated a second, as if struggling with himself as to what to do next. Hallie couldn't dart back inside, though that was very much what she wanted to do. Perhaps neither could Cam, because he started across the street toward her.

Her heart thudded erratically and her palms grew damp on the magazine. After Granny's court appearance was over, she could escape from here—and she wouldn't have to worry about sweating palms or racing heartbeats again. At least not around this man.

He looked beat, Hallie thought when he neared. Had he been working hard? His usual smile was absent, as if it took too much energy to bring it to life. His eyes were dark, hooded, but not as cold as on the day they'd argued. He searched her face, as if wanting to read something in it, something about her. What, she didn't know.

"Hello, Hallie," he said coolly.

"Cam." She didn't know how else to respond. Suddenly she didn't know what to say to this man she'd once talked with so easily.

"How's Pearl?" he asked.

"She's fine. We...she saw a lawyer the other day. Ward Buchanan. Thank you for the referral. We liked him. He seems very competent."

The conversation was as stiff as Hallie felt on the inside.

"Miss Hattie and the group paid me a little...visit at the jail the other night," he said. "I suppose that was *your* doing."

"My doing?"

Hallie's face held a hint of confusion, but Cam had learned not to trust her feign of innocence. Not anymore. "Yeah," he went on, "they wanted to be arrested, had their arms out for the cuffs, even demanded I fingerprint the lot of them."

Her eyes were wide, and he was certain he saw an unbidden smile edge to her lips. She thought it funny? Well, Cam hadn't thought so. The whole scene had made him look like some kind of Simon Legree.

Hell, maybe he was. His whole life in this town seemed to be arresting the older generation. That made him some kind of an ogre, didn't it?

"Cam, I had nothing to do with that. I told you I would talk to the ladies, and I did. I suggested they see Ward, or someone, in case there were charges against—'' She stopped. ''You…you didn't arrest them, did you?''

He crossed his arms over his chest. ''They insisted.''

''Cam!''

''Don't worry, I didn't handcuff them to the cell or anything. I released them—pending further investigation.'' He didn't know what he wanted to do with this case. Other than maybe make it go away.

She was still giving him a wary glance. He knew the look, the look that said he was an ogre. Like he'd thought—Simon Legree.

''The ladies are determined to stand with Pearl in this. They feel a certain…loyalty to her,'' he said.

''Yeah, well, Cam—maybe, just maybe, that's what I was feeling when I didn't rat on my grandmother.''

He nodded. ''And maybe I asked too much from you, Hallie. I know how you feel about Pearl.''

He studied her, his gaze raking over her, slowly, thoroughly, as if trying to decide something in his mind. Was loyalty so wrong? Hallie wondered.

Was she so wrong?

Just then Cam checked his watch. ''I'm late,'' he said. ''I have a baseball game to coach.''

Their conversation was over. Cam turned to leave and Hallie watched him head off for the vacant lot just past the square and the group of boys playing there, looking forward, she knew, to his expertise that he so generously shared.

There was a lot of good in Cam. He cared about this adopted town of his. He gave of himself to the residents and especially the kids. He coached their team, taught them fly-fishing, worried when they couldn't stay in school—yet when it came to a personal life of his own, a family, children... He didn't seem to want any of those things.

With a final glance at the man, and a deep sigh that rose up from her heart, she went back to reading her magazine—but she didn't see a thing on the page. There were too many tears in her eyes.

"You had words with the man," Granny said on the long drive home.

Hallie had felt her watchful gaze on her for the past few miles and suspected something like this was coming.

"We...we had a conversation. I wouldn't call it...*words.*"

"I would."

"Granny, please...I'm fine."

"Don't look fine to me."

She never gave up, Hallie thought, but Granny remained quiet the rest of the trip, and for that, Hallie was grateful.

That evening she washed up the supper dishes while Granny rested in her favorite old rocker. Sometimes Hallie forgot the woman didn't have the energy of a twenty-year-old.

"You're a good granddaughter, Hallie," Granny said as soon as Hallie had put away the last dish and draped Granny's embroidered dish towel over the rack to dry.

Hallie glanced at her grandmother, that lively face she had loved for years, those bony old arms that had hugged her as a child and made her feel secure, that wiry little body that had the strength of ten men. She hardly looked like the town's number-one public enemy tonight. She looked soft and wistful—and maybe a little vulnerable.

Hallie knew about vulnerable; she knew how much it could hurt. "I just did a few dishes," she replied.

Granny's gaze fixed on her fiercely. "I don't mean about the dishes. I mean about everything you done for me, Hallie. I might be cranky and crotchety sometimes, but I do 'preciate it all."

"Oh, Granny." She went to give her a hug. "I do it because I love you."

"I know that, child," she said, allowing the hug, then drew back and studied Hallie intently. "I made a fine mess of things here in this town," she said. "And I caused you pain, as well."

Hallie gave a small smile. "Only some worry, Granny. Worry about one little grandmother who's very special to me."

That didn't seem to satisfy Granny. Her gaze remained on Hallie's face. "And Cam Osborne," she said. "I caused you grief with him, too—and don't tell me I didn't. I saw you with him today. I couldn't hear what the two of you was sayin', but I didn't have to. I saw the way you was each lookin' at the other."

Hallie dropped her hands from her grandmother's shoulders. Did she think she could hide her feelings from this woman? Granny saw everything. But this time she was sticking her nose in where it wasn't needed.

"Granny, I told you my problems with Cam were my own folly. They had nothing to do with you."

Granny considered that for a long moment, but didn't look convinced. "All the same, I made a mess o' things around here when I didn't mean nobody any harm."

"I know you didn't, Granny Pearl."

Granny rocked quietly in her chair for another hour, a pensive crease added to the other fine wrinkles in her forehead, thinking her own thoughts, fretting in her own way, trying to find her own peace.

Cam heard Pearl's old clunker long before the woman bustled through the front door of his jail. Now what did the old bird want? he wondered.

He shoved aside his paperwork and offered her a chair.

She didn't take it.

"I won't be here that long, Sheriff. I just came to tell you I ain't got hard feelings. I know you was just doin' your duty, upholdin' the law, and I s'pose I can respect that. After all you're the sheriff around here."

Cam sat back down, a little surprised at the woman. He'd have expected her to come after him with one of her old iron skillets, rather than this offering of peace.

"I appreciate that, Pearl."

"I'm sorry, too, for all those mean things I said about you. You're a fine man, Cam Osborne— maybe a little hardheaded, but that trait you ain't got no lock on. You're good with the little ones 'round here, too, and that goes a long way in my book."

"Thanks, Pearl. Coming from you that means a lot."

He meant it. He liked the old gal—he always had. She could be a trial—and he was certain she gave Hallie more than a few cares—but she meant well.

"I don't know what went on between you and my Hallie—the girl won't talk about it. But she's determined to leave here when my case is settled and take me with her. An' if that's what she wants to do, I won't balk about goin'. My Hallie is a good person, and I know she's just got my good interests at heart."

Cam couldn't answer. His heart had dropped to the pit of his stomach—and he wasn't sure he could breathe, much less get words out.

Hallie was going to leave here—and Pearl had agreed to go with her. There'd be nothing to keep her here now, not if Pearl wasn't offering resistance.

Cam had never felt so blasted miserable in his life.

Not even back in Chicago when all his belief systems had crashed into shards. Hallie had the ability to hurt him more than anything he'd gone through then, he realized—and he didn't know what the hell to do about it.

When he recovered his aplomb, Pearl had sashayed out. She'd muttered something more to him—but what it was, he hadn't heard.

All he knew was that his life was disintegrating, and it was all his own fault.

Chapter Eleven

Why was it a man had to lose something before he realized what he'd lost was what he most wanted in the world?

Cam had lost Hallie—truly lost her.

She'd be leaving here soon—and with Granny going with her, there'd be no reason for her to return. Without Hallie around, the little town he'd grown to love would lose its sparkle.

So would his life, he realized even more glumly.

And all because he was a muleheaded idiot. All because he hadn't seen Hallie's side in this. All he'd seen was his own.

He needed to talk to her, he needed to apologize before it was too late.

He didn't have too high a hope of getting her to stick around this little burg. She'd made it clear from the start that she'd be going home to Fort Worth, to her teaching job at that school with all the advantages. He didn't have a prayer's hope of convincing her to stay and offer a few of those advantages to the kids around here.

He didn't have a prayer's hope of convincing her to marry him.

But he could apologize—he owed her that.

That night after he'd showered and shaved and rehearsed forty versions of an apology to his bathroom mirror, he jerked on a pair of chino slacks and a good shirt and rode off to tilt at windmills.

The little cabin in Pearl's neck of the woods gleamed like a soft beacon in the night, warm and secure. Would Pearl really pack up the past seventy-nine years of her life and leave here with Hallie?

If it was what Hallie wanted she would, he realized. Hadn't Pearl told him just that this afternoon?

He climbed out of the Cherokee, feeling his palms sweat and his throat grow tight. In two days Judge McBain would be hearing Pearl's case, and soon after that, Hallie would leave.

But he didn't want to think about that, didn't want to think how that would affect him, how empty his life would suddenly be.

Alone—that was what he'd wanted when he first came here to Greens Hollow. Now it was the last thing he thought he could endure.

Hallie came to the door when he knocked. The light from the room beyond backlit her small frame, her cloud of red hair, her fragile shoulders. He couldn't read her face, her eyes, know whether she was glad to see him or wanted him to leave. At least she didn't invite him to do the latter.

He felt a certain relief in that.

"Hallie…" The knot in his throat tightened. "Can we talk for a few minutes?" An hour. A lifetime.

How could he let her walk out of his life? But if her life in Fort Worth was what she wanted, really wanted…

He couldn't let himself think about that.

She stepped out onto the porch, into the spill of moonlight and took a seat on one of the chairs. Cam found the porch railing and rested one hip against it.

She was dressed in a pair of soft-washed white jeans and a pale peach top that hugged her breasts. The peach hue, mingled with the moonlight from above, gave a delicate glow to her face. Her green eyes were wide and solemn.

What he'd rehearsed earlier had fled his mind. He didn't know what to say, except to let her know he'd been a lunkhead.

"I came to tell you I was wrong the other day. I shouldn't have blasted you about…withholding facts. I didn't look at your side of it, didn't realize you were only doing what you felt you needed to do—protect your grandmother." From the mean, bad sheriff, he thought to himself. The *uncompromising* sheriff. "I'd asked too much of you, Hallie, asked the impossible—and I shouldn't have."

"Apology accepted," she said softly, graciously—more graciously than he deserved. "I didn't mean to hold out on you about…anything, Cam. Not really. I thought I could handle it myself. Then…the men got drunk and landed in your jail, and I knew I hadn't done a very good job of it."

"Yeah, well, *that's* a night to forget. But everybody lived through it and the men got their punishment—they ended up with roaring hangovers. They won't do that again soon.''

She smiled. ''Now that Granny's shut down,'' she said.

He studied her for a long moment, thinking how very beautiful she looked, how soft, how...tempting. ''Pearl's lucky she has you, lucky she has someone who'd fight tooth and nail for her, who's loyal to a fault.''

He realized it was what he loved about her. He wondered what it would be like to have her fight that way for him.

''Cam, Granny's agreed to go back with me after her court appearance—providing the judge will allow it.''

Cam felt the knife turn in him the way it had earlier today when Pearl had broken the news. It wasn't any less painful the second time. In fact, it was worse. This time it was from Hallie's own lips.

''Then I hope the judge refuses to let her leave the county.''

One eyebrow shot up in surprise.

''So you won't leave here and never come back,'' he explained.

''Cam, I have school to teach. And the change will be good for Granny.''

But not for him—and he'd bet not good for Pearl, either. As for Hallie, he wished she could be happy here, wished he could *make* her happy.

''There's a need for a teacher right here, Hallie,'' he said. ''If you'd consider it.''

She studied him, her eyes wide, curious, then she glanced down at her hands, tangling them in her lap.

"I can't stay here." Her voice was low, soft. He could barely hear her. "I can't stay here any more than you could have stayed in Chicago, Cam."

"What do you mean?"

She stood up and walked to the end of the porch, hugging her arms as if the warm night air had suddenly turned frigid.

"I was hurt by this town once before," she said quietly. "I'd come to stay with Granny Pearl for the summer and fell in love—or what I thought was love." She drew a breath. "I was seventeen; he was nineteen. When...when I found I was pregnant I foolishly thought we'd marry. I...knew I wanted children, lots of them."

"What happened, Hallie?"

"He didn't share the dreams I had. I—I left here and—" her voice broke "—I lost the baby."

He went to her then, took her in his arms and held her, just held her.

He whispered soft things to her, inane things—it didn't matter what. As long as she knew he was there, that he cared.

When her crying turned to soft snuffles, she drew away from him. "It was a long time ago. But coming back here—"

She wouldn't want to stay here; he understood that now. This was just a town—and a town couldn't hurt you, but he knew Hallie didn't see it that way. Wouldn't.

"I'm glad you told me," he said.

She tried to brush aside her tears, but failed miserably. "It seems we've both had a few bruises along the way," she remarked.

"Yeah."

He drew her to him and planted one chaste kiss on her lips. With the flat of his thumb he dried the tears she'd missed.

"That's why you teach, isn't it?" he said. Hallie loved children—and she hadn't been able to have the child she wanted very much.

She nodded. "We all find ways to compensate for our losses," she said quietly.

And Cam would soon have his loss. Hallie.

A woman who'd come to mean more to him than life itself.

He leaned his head down and kissed her, really kissed her this time, drinking her in, fearing it would be the last time, the last taste of her he'd ever sample.

She was liquid in his arms, soft and fluid as the night that surrounded them. And he wanted the moment to go on forever.

But Hallie was leaving here. And right or wrong, it was what she wanted. He couldn't propose to her, ask her to stay and marry him. What if he, too, ended up smashing her dreams? That he couldn't bear.

From somewhere in the far reaches of his mind he thought he heard a door open, heard Pearl clear her throat. Then the door closed again.

Slowly, reluctantly, Hallie drew away. "I think that was Granny Pearl," she said.

"Did she go for a shotgun?"

He saw her smile, a small wistful one. "I'm going to miss you, Cam Osborne," she said.

That wasn't half of what Cam knew *he* had to endure.

* * *

Hallie had Granny Pearl to think about and Granny's appearance before Judge McBain. She had no time to give to thoughts of Cam and their talk last night, no time to give to how much she'd miss him when she got back to Fort Worth.

He'd wanted her to stay here—but how could she do that? This town reminded her of too much—he'd understood that. He didn't want marriage, children. She recalled there'd been no proposal laced through their conversation. Only an apology and a plea for her to stay and open the school. Though that was a noble thought, Hallie had kids to teach back home.

And Granny would be going with her—if the judge was lenient.

Hallie was worried about that, worried that her spirited grandmother might turn the courtroom on its ear. Granny needed to appear civil, sedate and, above all, *contrite*. No reminders she'd once powdered the eminent judge's bottom. No mumbo jumbo that her squeezins were a cure-all for "rheumatiz" or anything else. The judge wouldn't buy any of it.

Hallie's own needs, her jumbled feelings about Cam, were secondary right now. She needed to keep her mind on Granny until after the court hearing, until Granny's fate was decided.

Cam was seated in the section of McBain's courtroom reserved for witnesses. He was pretty much it—except for a character witness or two that Ward Buchanan had tucked away should he need them, someone who'd say that Pearl Cates was a model citizen, an asset to the community.

Since he was the arresting officer it was his duty

to give the details of the arrest and the charges against Granny Pearl—not something he was looking forward to doing, even though the woman had broken the law.

He glanced up at the sound of the courtroom door opening. Pearl had arrived, flanked on one side by Hallie, appearing in control and ready for battle, and on the other by Pearl's five cohorts-in-crime, appearing equally determined. Only Pearl looked defeated. She'd lost her starch, her rancor, her churlishness—and Cam wasn't sure that was a good thing.

In the two years he'd lived here, he'd never seen her like this. What was the matter, was she afraid of the judge? He scoffed. The woman could face a grizzly and not be afraid.

He'd bet his badge she was in the doldrums because Hallie intended to take her to Fort Worth with her, take her from this world she loved and knew.

Couldn't Hallie see what she was doing to Granny Pearl? She'd be ripping the woman's heart out if they left here. She'd be ripping *his* heart out, as well.

And Cam had done very little to stop her.

Oh, he'd suggested she stay and reopen the school, but he'd held back on making any big declarations of love.

What's the matter, Cam? Afraid to make that final commitment? To trust in someone again?

To run a risk again?

He'd refused to consider falling in love a second time—afraid it wouldn't last. Afraid that when it didn't, he'd hurt like before. But Hallie wasn't Elise, he knew. She was different. Neither was she like his partner. She hadn't betrayed him with Pearl; she'd only done what she'd had to do—protect her own.

It was part of why he loved her, part of why he wanted her, *why he couldn't let her go.*

Just then court was called to order, the Honorable Judge Wilson McBain presiding. There were three or four cases to dispense with first—minor things, none of them involving the Sheriff's Office. Cam was glad; he could keep his thoughts on Pearl's case.

He saw Hallie fidget in her seat, anxious for the judge to work through the morning's docket. Beside her, Pearl sat stoic and silent, too silent—at least for Granny Pearl.

Finally with the next bang of the gavel it was their turn. The judge called the key players before the bench and the proceedings began. Cam stated that the charges of the court against Granny were accurate. Yes, he'd found a still, fully operable—and recently used—on her property. Yes, he'd taken several bottles of moonshine into evidence at the same time.

The judge requested a look at the evidence in question, took a whiff from one of the bottles, then narrowed his eyes at the defendant. "What have you got to say for yourself, Pearl?"

She didn't wait for her lawyer to answer on her behalf. "Guilty, your honor."

"I see. And what about the still. Was it yours, as well?"

"Yes, sir," came the feeble, small voice.

Cam shifted, uncomfortable with this new Granny. Even Hallie looked concerned.

"And where is said still now?" McBain asked.

Hallie answered. "It's dismantled, Your Honor, and locked away in the trunk of my car."

The judge peered curiously at her. "And do you plan to take responsibility for disposing of it?" he asked.

Hallie nodded. "Yes, Your Honor. I'm also willing to take full responsibility for my grandmother's well-being, if Your Honor will show leniency. I would like to take her back to Fort Worth to live with me."

Before McBain could reply, Granny answered. "Won't go."

Cam wanted to cheer, he wanted to slap the old girl on the back, he wanted to give her one great big smackeroo on her wrinkled old cheek.

"I'm sorry, Hallie," she said. "I know what you want, but I'm stickin' right here, thank you." She turned to the judge. "Now just give me my punishment, whatever it is."

At that everyone began to speak at once—Hallie insisting the subject of Granny going with her had been settled, the attorney wanting a moment to talk with his client, five prim but vociferous ladies advancing toward the bench, demanding equal punishment with Pearl, and the judge banging the gavel for quiet in the courtroom.

"My two babies," Granny said as George and Myrtle loped over to see what it was she'd brought them for their noon meal. "Hallie, give Myrtle some biscuit," Granny ordered. "The buttermilk's her favorite."

The old girl seemed to be herself now that she'd

escaped the courtroom. Hallie smiled as she watched her grandmother chuck the creatures under their be-whiskered chins. "Pearl's not goin' off to the jail-house, after all," she crooned to the two. "Not goin' to Texas, neither. I'm stayin' right here with you."

It was true, the judge had let Granny Pearl off with the understanding that she never again engage in the distilling of spirits and a stern warning that should she, or the other town ladies, ever show up in his courtroom again he'd throw the book at them, no questions asked.

Hallie was pleased with the outcome—but not with Granny's declaration that she wasn't going with her. One look at the determined set of her grand-mother's shoulders, however, had told her there was little use arguing. The woman had made up her mind.

She supposed Cam had been right. She couldn't take Granny Pearl away from her home.

Hallie fed George some biscuit too, while Granny dished leftover stew into their feeding tins. Soon the two goats were feasting greedily, and Granny wiped her hands on her old print apron.

Hallie would miss having the woman with her in Fort Worth. She also knew she'd be making frequent trips to Greens Hollow to see her and be sure she was getting along all right alone.

That would mean seeing Cam again—but she sup-posed that couldn't be helped.

Cam. He'd been a real help today in the court-room. As sheriff he'd given his testimony, then in a surprise turn had asked the judge to consider allow-ing Granny a second chance. If he knew Pearl Cates like he thought he did, he'd added, the judge wouldn't be disappointed.

Cam's statement had carried a lot of weight, Hallie was sure. And she owed him a debt of gratitude. He hadn't needed to say that, hadn't needed to do more than give his usual testimony about the arrest.

"What's the matter, you moonin' over that man again?" Granny had finished with her two babies and decided to divert full attention now to Hallie. "If you had a lick of sense, girl, you'd marry him. I know he done asked you to stay."

"Granny…" Hallie glanced at her in surprise— and a little irritation. "I thought you didn't like Cam."

"We made our peace—and the stubborn fool's in love with you. Anybody with two eyes can see that."

Hallie wasn't at all sure about that, but the possibility gave her a thrill just the same. Then reason set in. This was Cam they were talking about, a man who wanted to go it on his own in the future.

And Hallie wanted something entirely different.

"Granny, Cam did ask me to stay—but it was to reopen the school—not to marry him."

Granny waved her hand as if that were only a minor drawback.

Her grandmother saw things so simply sometimes—and life was far from simple. "I'm afraid Cam isn't looking for a wife," she explained. "He doesn't want to marry, and he…he doesn't want children."

"Poppycock! I seen him with the little 'uns in this town. He doesn't look like a man who wouldn't love a *passel* o' kids."

Granny had that wrong—dead wrong. She remembered what he'd told her, that it was fortunate he and Elise hadn't had children. That kids deserved more than a broken marriage—and trouble in their life. Cam didn't believe in marriage, had no intention of going that road again.

He may have been attracted to Hallie, but love, the kind that led down the aisle to the altar...? Sadly, that wasn't Cam.

"What makes you so all-fired sure, girl? He tell you that?"

Granny wasn't giving up this conversation easily. "Yes, Granny, as a matter of fact, he did."

"Lately?"

How had they gotten on the subject, anyway? Granny was like a dog worrying a bone when she got on a topic that interested her, *made her curious.* But Hallie would just as soon drop the whole discussion.

"Granny..." She laced her voice with exasperation.

"Well, was it?"

"No, not lately, but—"

"There, see? You don't know a thing."

Hallie wished Granny was right. She'd even given some small thought to Cam's suggestion she reopen the town school, be the teacher they couldn't get, but Cam didn't want her in the way she wanted him to.

And staying here under those circumstances would be too painful. Even knowing she'd be here for Granny didn't alter that fact. Hallie would just plain hurt, every day of her life.

And she'd remember the child she lost, too. She'd

have children in her life, under her care, but none of her own to hold in her arms, to love as only a mother loved.

"Granny, I'm going back to Fort Worth. Tonight. But I promise I'll come to visit. I won't stay away like I did before."

That afternoon as Hallie packed she ran across the letters from her small pupils, the goodbye letters. She cherished each and every one of the children, but she knew they'd be going on to third grade, then fourth. They loved her, wanted her for their teacher next year, but that wasn't the way the school system worked.

They'd have a new teacher and Hallie would have new students—always new students.

Was it so wrong to want children of her very own, marriage, a husband to share her life with, to grow old with?

She wanted those things. And she wanted them with Cam.

"But that part won't happen," she said aloud, then tossed the precious letters back in the suitcase and clicked it shut.

Chapter Twelve

Cam drove the Cherokee flat out, careening around curves and topping hills at unaccustomed speed. He'd done some tall thinking since leaving the courtroom this morning—and he was damned shaky about the decision he'd come to.

But now that his mind was made up—right or wrong—he had to talk to Hallie. And he feared she might already have packed up and headed for Fort Worth.

She hadn't been too happy about Pearl's decision to stick to her guns and stay; she might have lit out of here in a bit of a pique at her grandmother.

Well, if she had, he'd just have to drive all the way to Texas to tell her how he felt about her.

Hell, he'd even consider going back to work as a big-city cop in that danged town of hers if that's what he had to do.

Cam groaned at that thought. He liked Greens

Hollow, liked being his own boss, liked not having a partner. And Hallie, whether she realized it or not, was sorely needed here. *He* needed her, too.

That was the conclusion he'd come to—the conclusion he would have realized had he not been so damned hardheaded.

She was there. Cam saw her car parked behind Granny's green battlewagon and deftly pulled in behind it.

As he rounded her car he couldn't resist a check inside to see if it was packed and loaded for a trip down the highway. It wasn't, but that didn't mean her luggage wasn't in the trunk.

No one came out on the porch to greet him, but he knew Hallie had to be there.

Were she and Granny discussing the outcome of the case? Talking about Hallie leaving, Granny Pearl staying, and how each felt about it? Would Pearl be trying to convince her to come back for visits?

Cam rapped on the front door, then paced nervously. There was an old board loose on the porch. Cam could fix it for Pearl. He made a mental note to do that at the first opportunity.

It seemed forever—but was actually only seconds—before Hallie drew the door open. She looked beautiful wearing a yellow sun dress that showed off her curves. So beautiful he ached inside.

"Cam?"

She seemed surprised to see him. Pleasantly? "I was hoping you hadn't already packed up and gone," he said.

"Did you come to see Granny, then?"

Hell, no. "I came to see *you.*"

Hallie felt her heart trip and stumble. It had already picked up its pace just seeing him standing there on the front porch. She'd hoped he might seek her out.

If he hadn't she was going to stop by the sheriff's office later today to thank him for taking up Granny's cause with the judge. And to say goodbye.

She knew she couldn't leave without doing so.

"Is the old girl napping?"

Not by a long shot, Hallie thought. If she knew Granny she had her ear pitched, waiting to pick up this conversation like she was equipped with radar. She'd done nothing but bend Hallie's ear about the man all afternoon.

"She's very much awake, I'm afraid."

She stepped out on the porch and pulled the door closed. She didn't know why Cam had come—but whatever they said to one another was private conversation. She'd decide later whether to tell Granny about it.

Any of it.

"That's what I thought." Cam hadn't missed the way Hallie had closed the door behind her. Old pitchers had big ears... "I brought you this," he said, handing her a small red rose. He wanted to give her more. He wanted to give her the world.

"Thank you," she said softly. She brought it to her nose and sniffed its fragrance.

They sauntered off the porch and onto Granny's lawn, out of the woman's earshot. Birds chirped noisily overhead; the air was redolent with the scent of honeysuckle.

"I—I was coming by later to tell you goodbye,"

she said as they walked. "And to thank you for what you did for Granny today. I appreciate it."

Cam didn't hear a word past goodbye. "You're intending to leave then?"

"Cam, we…we had this discussion, remember?"

He remembered. "I remember that I didn't finish it," he said, pulling her to a stop beside him. "I remember there was one hell of a lot I left unsaid."

Hallie looked up at him. He stood tall and determined, towering over her. Her heart thudded heavily in her chest at just the sight of him. The wind had tousled his hair. The afternoon sun bronzed his arms.

It seemed forever since Granny's appearance before the judge this morning. A lot had changed since then. Or had it remained the same? Hallie was going back to teach another year. Her life would go on as before. Granny would still be here—so many miles away.

And so would Cam.

Only now she'd have memories of him to haunt her—his touch, his kisses, his delicious male scent, the heat in his eyes, the smile she loved to see form on his sexy mouth when he was amused or pleased or happy.

At the moment the smile was missing.

"Unsaid, such as…?"

A squirrel skittered up a tree. "I've had time to think, Hallie. After…after Chicago I'd set new rules for myself. I'd decided no entanglements—especially the kind that had to do with falling in love. I'd decided that wasn't for me. But then…you came along, Hallie—and those rules turned fuzzy in my mind.''

Hallie's breath hitched. ''What are you saying, Cam?''

''I'm saying, I broke those rules. Maybe it was from that first kiss, maybe it was from the first time I *saw* you—I don't know. All I know was I fell in love with you when I'd promised myself I wouldn't.''

It was what Hallie had most wanted to hear from Cam. That he loved her. It was what she felt for him, too. But she knew how he felt about marriage, about children. Had *those* rules changed as well?

She didn't think she could stand to hear him say he loved her only to find out the rules that mattered most to her hadn't been a part of it.

She put her hands to her ears, as if she could shut out his words. ''Don't say any more, Cam.''

He studied her face, that face he wanted to stroke, caress, the mouth he wanted to plunder, then drew her hands down, holding them captive with his own. ''Are you telling me you don't feel the same way, Hallie—because if you are, then I've just made a major fool of myself here.''

She shook her head. ''I'm not saying that.'' She'd never say that. She loved Cam with her very soul. ''I—I'm saying it wouldn't work between us.''

She pulled free from Cam and took a few steps away. He followed and grasped her shoulders, spinning her to face him. His face looked stricken, as stricken as she felt on the inside. Why did love have to hurt so much? Why did love have to be so complicated?

"It's the town—isn't it? *This* town—there's not enough here for you. No...advantages."

"No, Cam. It isn't that."

"What, then?" He saw the pain in Hallie's green eyes, then he remembered what she'd told him the other night, about how she'd fallen in love here once—with that jerk who didn't appreciate what he had. The baby. The baby she'd lost. Oh, Lord, that's what it was. "It is the town—but not for that reason. It's what happened here before. Hallie, if that's it, I can move to Fort Worth. I want you—I don't know how much clearer I can make it."

"You belong here, Cam."

"And you belong in Texas? Hell, Hallie—that's not at all what I had in mind."

She had to say it. She had to make him understand, even if the tears came and she looked all bloaty-faced and red-eyed and he'd forever remember how she looked the last time he saw her. "Cam, ever since I lost the baby I've wanted nothing more than to have another, lots of babies. I wanted marriage and kids and a live-happily-ever-after life. I realize now that I don't care where that is—Fort Worth or...or the moon, but it's what I want."

"Hell, woman, that's what I'm offering you—unless I'm not the man you want that happily ever after and all those kids with."

Hallie wasn't sure she'd heard him right. Maybe it was a trick of her wishful imagination, maybe she'd just plain heard him *wrong.* "But you'd said... Elise...your marriage... You...you didn't want kids of your own, you'd been glad there hadn't been any. They'd have been...complications—"

"I was glad Elise and I hadn't had kids, but that doesn't go for how I feel *now*—about you."

"Now? You mean that's one of the rules you're willing to bend?"

"More than bend. Hallie, if you'll have me, I'll snap that rule right in two."

He looked so expectant, waiting for her to say the words, she had to tamp down the laugh that threatened to erupt and destroy this moment. "Cam, I love you."

He went down on one knee before her.

"Then marry me, Hallie. Be my wife, have those babies you want with me."

"Cam, what are you saying?"

"I'm saying I want you in my life, Hallie. Anyway that we can be together."

Tears misted her eyes. She vaguely saw him remove a tiny box from his pocket. One delicate diamond ring nestled inside. Hallie knew he meant every word. He'd come here expecting her to say yes, to marry him.

She brushed aside a tear. "Oh, yes, Cam. Yes, I'll marry you—and we can live right here. I've done some thinking about that. This town needs a school—and I have a lot of ideas I can bring here."

He stood up. "And I'd love to hear all about them, too, woman—but first I want to kiss you."

She went into his arms, arms that felt so right, so wonderful, and when his lips met hers, she knew there was nothing more she wanted from life.

"I'm ready to start working on this parenthood thing anytime you are," he said, nipping her neck in sensual little kisses that she knew would be her undoing.

Epilogue

Granny Pearl walked Hallie down the aisle of the small church in Greens Hollow. Hallie hadn't wanted to be married anywhere else.

She'd come home.

Her painful memories of the town no longer tortured her. She'd come to terms with them, thanks in part to Cam, in part to Granny Pearl.

Her grandmother's steps were sure and nimble, and there was a beatific smile on her aging face, a solemnity Hallie only hoped lasted through the reception that followed. She didn't want to think her feisty relative might do something foolish, like spiking the punch with some leftover bottle of her local lightning.

Granny and her five wayward pals *were* in charge of the refreshments, she remembered with sudden unease.

A small frown of worry pleated her forehead.

Hallie wanted Cam all to herself on their wedding night—not down at the jail locking up one little group of troublesome seniors.

Just then she glanced up and saw Cam waiting for her at the edge of the altar—and all thoughts of Granny and her impossible mischief fled her mind. Cam was all she could think about, the man she loved with her entire heart and soul.

He smiled and Hallie stepped forward, ready to become his wife—but not before Granny had one final word of warning for the sheriff.

"Cam Osborne, you'd better be good to my Hallie or you'll find yourself picking a peck of buckshot from that handsome backside of yours."

Cam looked for all the world like he adored the ornery half-pint of a woman—and Hallie realized he did. He also loved Hallie, a knowledge she treasured more and more each day.

He grinned over at the feisty old woman. "Don't you worry about that, Pearl. I aim to make that pretty granddaughter of yours *very* happy."

Granny harumphed loudly, then kissed Hallie softly on the cheek and took her place in the front pew. Hallie smiled up at Cam as he took her hand in his. "I love you, Cam Osborne," she whispered softly.

"Not half as much as I love you, Hallie Cates."

The ceremony began, but Hallie barely heard the minister's words.

Cam's rang in her heart.

*   *   *   *   *

Silhouette ROMANCE™

If you enjoyed what you just read,
then we've got an offer you can't resist!

Take 2 bestselling love stories FREE!

Plus get a FREE surprise gift!

Clip this page and mail it to Silhouette Reader Service™

IN U.S.A.	IN CANADA
3010 Walden Ave.	P.O. Box 609
P.O. Box 1867	Fort Erie, Ontario
Buffalo, N.Y. 14240-1867	L2A 5X3

YES! Please send me 2 free Silhouette Romance® novels and my free surprise gift. Then send me 6 brand-new novels every month, which I will receive months before they're available in stores. In the U.S.A., bill me at the bargain price of $2.90 plus 25¢ delivery per book and applicable sales tax, if any*. In Canada, bill me at the bargain price of $3.25 plus 25¢ delivery per book and applicable taxes**. That's the complete price and a savings of over 10% off the cover prices—what a great deal! I understand that accepting the 2 free books and gift places me under no obligation ever to buy any books. I can always return a shipment and cancel at any time. Even if I never buy another book from Silhouette, the 2 free books and gift are mine to keep forever. So why not take us up on our invitation. You'll be glad you did!

215 SEN CNE7
315 SEN CNE9

Name	(PLEASE PRINT)	
Address	Apt.#	
City	State/Prov.	Zip/Postal Code

* Terms and prices subject to change without notice. Sales tax applicable in N.Y.
** Canadian residents will be charged applicable provincial taxes and GST.
   All orders subject to approval. Offer limited to one per household.
   ® are registered trademarks of Harlequin Enterprises Limited.

SROM99   ©1998 Harlequin Enterprises Limited

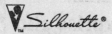
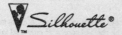

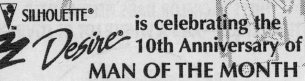
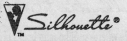

THESE BACHELOR DADS NEED A LITTLE TENDERNESS—AND A WHOLE LOT OF LOVING!

January 1999—A Rugged Ranchin' Dad
by Kia Cochrane (SR# 1343)
Tragedy had wedged Stone Tyler's family apart. Now this rugged rancher would do everything in his power to be the perfect daddy—and recapture his wife's heart—before time ran out....

April 1999 —Prince Charming's Return
by Myrna Mackenzie (SR# 1361)
Gray Alexander was back in town—and had just met the son he had never known he had. Now he wanted to make Cassie Pratt pay for her deception eleven years ago...even if the price was marriage!

And in June 1999 don't miss Donna Clayton's touching story of Dylan Minster, a man who has been raising his daughter all alone....

Fall in love with our FABULOUS FATHERS!

And look for more FABULOUS FATHERS in the months to come. Only from

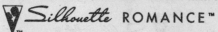

Silhouette ROMANCE™

Available wherever Silhouette books are sold.

Look us up on-line at: http://www.romance.net

SRFFJ-J